RUMOR 1, 2, 3

Nancy Oleksy

ISBN 979-8-88851-115-2 (Paperback)
ISBN 979-8-88851-116-9 (Digital)

First Edition

Covenant Books
11661 Hwy 707
Murrells Inlet, SC 29576
www.covenantbooks.com

RUMOR 1

CHAPTER 1

The Rumor Comes to Life

Like most days, my desk was piled high with things to do. There were articles to proofread that were definitely front-page material and recipes to edit for "filler" columns. There were baby announcements and wedding pictures to send back to the photo booth for processing and banners to lay out on empty pages that wouldn't be empty by the five o'clock press time. As I pulled off my coat and hung it on the hook behind my desk, I shoved my purse into the bottom drawer of my desk. "Thus starts another day as the community news editor," I said quietly to myself as I glanced around the office of our small-town newspaper.

It was actually a really great job, even if Ron had forgotten to turn on the copying machine for the ten-millionth time, and JoAnn was already standing behind my desk, getting warm by the portable heater I kept there to take the autumn chill off. I didn't mind that she stood there for warmth, but she had this habit of constantly humming. It was very distracting when I was trying to watch our editor Charlie's spelling and grammar and "flow" in his articles. But it would be awfully mean to shoo her away to her chilly office in the nearly hundred-year-old building.

When the first phone call came in a few minutes before the office was to open, I debated if I should pick it up. Well, why not? I was here. There was a vibrant show of oranges and reds and spicy browns out there on our trees with a gorgeous blue sky and a little breeze that made a few of the leaves begin to flutter down to the ground. The kids were safely delivered to their school, and I remembered to lock the doors at the house. All seemed right with my world, so I picked up the phone.

"*The Bulletin*, it's a great day! How can I help you?" I thought I seemed especially cheerful.

"*Why do you hate men?*" screamed the rough voice on the other end of the line.

Stunned, I hesitated.

Again, the voice rang clear, "*I said, why do you hate men*?"

Pretty quickly, my Italian temper got simmering.

I thought rather quickly, *Well, I don't hate men…just you*. But instead, I said, "Whatever do you mean, sir?"

"You fail to put the men's bowling scores into the paper! You only put in the women's scores! To me, that means you hate men!"

It was another one of "those" comments from an uninformed subscriber. I got these all the time. For a town that was mostly a friendly place, a few people could sure get their panties in a knot over some very small details.

Recognizing the man's voice as Arnie Reynolds, our seemingly lonely widower on Fourth Street, I pulled back my intended Italian emotional response and said, "Arnie, I put the women's bowling scores in the paper because Ann Marie—you know Ann Marie—well, she brings in a list of the ladies scores *before* the deadline for the Tuesday paper. And remember, that's the only edition our publisher allows for bowling scores. Your men's teams miss the deadline all the time, even when I have reminded you. In fact, last week, *nobody* brought in *any* men's scores!"

He hesitated for just a moment and then continued, "Well, you should put the men's scores in as much as the women's."

"Well, you should bring them to me by the deadline, and I will," I said.

And with that, he slammed down his phone and was gone. Even if I was one to drink coffee, which I wasn't, this conversation had already gotten my blood pumping. Who needs coffee?

With a day starting off like this one, I half expected it to blow sky-high by day's end, but surprisingly, things went along pretty smoothly. JoAnn went back to her office, and I was minus the litany of unrecognizable tunes. The evening edition was coming together with some pretty interesting content and good-quality photos. And lunch with my four best buddies was only two hours away.

I was a pretty lucky woman, really. Well, at least in this part of my life, I was feeling lucky. I had two great teenage kids or as they liked to remind me, "almost adults," but great all the same. I enjoyed a good job, a nice-enough home, friends, and a terrific extended family, although they were in other states. I analyzed myself from time to time and thought I was pretty balanced spiritually, emotionally, mentally (thank goodness), and physically. So I had no complaints... at least today.

The morning raced by, and before I knew it, I was hurrying to the "Golden Girdle." It was really the Golden Grill, but my editor, Charlie, always called it the Golden Girdle. This was due to the fact it was our town's largest and most popular lunch spot, and it served humongous servings of everything. People tended to always overeat there, and as Charlie says, "They need girdles to roll outta there." He had an astute power of observation as most people could not resist the aromas and tempting descriptions of each day's special.

The other lunch place favorite was a little piece of midday heaven owned by Tony and Anna, our resident Italian chefs. Tony loved to bake all sorts of wonderful things from bread to almond biscotti, and Anna was a whiz at tender meats, sauces, and mouthfuls of all things scrumptious. Today was Golden Grill day.

My friends had all beat me to the restaurant and had "steaked" out our table. Yes, I said "steaked" because there was no way Jackie, who worked in the mayor's office, would eat anything but a slab of beef these days! Luckily, the Golden Grill always had the best roast beef every day. Jackie was on a high-protein diet, and we all expected her to turn into a Guernsey before long. Jackie knew all the ins and outs of our town and was always a good source of intel for us. She kept us apprised of the workings of the mayor's office, he being an aloof kind of guy. We all thought he was perhaps somewhat "secretive," but about what, we could only speculate. Jackie and her hubby, Jack, had been married for a long time and had grown kids and several grandkids that they adored. Their grandkids thought it was most entertaining to have Grandpa Jack and Grandma Jackie around.

I waved to them as I wiped my very cute short boots on the door mat and made my way to the table. Janna was there, another newspaper employee. She worked in the ad department and could sell Old Mother Hubbard at least twelve more children. Janna was happily married to her high school sweetheart, and they had six kids. How she kept them all going was a marvel to me. Janna had worked at the newspaper for quite a while and was a trusted and valued employee by everyone. She had a great personality and kept the office atmosphere cheery and fun. I was so glad she was my friend.

Then there was Shelly, a stay-at-home mom with three rambunctious little *girls*—yes, girls! Boys are generally known for their wild and crazy antics, but not one boy in town could hold a candle to these three. That's probably why Shelly always seemed a little frazzled. We usually overlooked her mismatched shoes or socks. No one in her family seemed to mind the constant mess in every room of her house. Her husband was a hardworking construction guy and was in constant demand from neighbors to help them with their projects.

My fourth best buddy was Trish. She was always the quiet one with a half-smile, sloping shoulders, and heavy sighs. She wore big coats, trying to make us think it was those coats that weighed her down. She lived alone, worked at the quilt store, and had a cat. Being a dog person, I was convinced it was the cat that had cast her gloomy spell over Trish. If we could just get rid of that cat, perhaps give it to the traveling gypsies, Trish was bound to feel better, right? I felt kind of sorry for Trish sometimes and so wished some wonderful, happy situation would open up for her.

Before long, we had all obtained our yummy nourishment for the day and settled down to the important work of finding out each other's business. I was in a listening and laughing mode and tuned into Janna's discussion of Jake from the hardware store who wanted a big holiday ad for an everyday price. Jake regularly wanted a "good deal" from Janna for his advertising, and she did her best to oblige.

Everybody in town used the hardware store for everything, and Jake could find a way to get even the tiniest part for some obscure farm implement for you. Jake and his hardware store were invaluable to our rural town.

I loved our hardware store too. My favorite parts of any hardware store were the bins of nails and screws. When I was young and went to the hardware store with my dad, I'd run my hands deep into the bins and let the big old nails and long screws fall from my little hands. I just couldn't make a trip to Jake's without at least one hand diving into a bin. As the only hardware store in town, Jake didn't really need to advertise. However, this year, there might be some kind of new fancy-dancy tool or a specialty thingamajig that would make the perfect gift. This possibility was what started the big discussion with Janna about an extra festive holiday ad.

Shelly then entertained us with the antics of her three little "darlings." They had decided to make their own soap, shampoo, and perfume. Their so-cool design catch was that it would only need to be one product. They could save their mom and dad lots of money this way. So they began collecting the scummy leftover bubbles from the ends of their baths in a large, empty former lotion bottle. And hey, some extra lotion in there would make everything smooth and soft, so let's add that, they thought! And for a while, they also collected the tiny shards of the bar soaps when they got too small to be of much use. I can hear them now. "Let's put these in there too."

Well, "collecting" took quite a number of weeks, and so they had just screwed on the top of the lotion bottle and set it on the window sill behind the curtain in their bedroom. It could "develop" there, they said.

They were awfully smart little girls and decided that one day, they better test their product. Shelly should have been somewhat suspicious when they *volunteered* to take a bath together to save water. They used their product on their hair and skin. It worked marvelously well, and they liked the aroma too. They apparently decided to try it again tomorrow before they told Mom.

Tomorrow's bath with their invention never came because the next morning found all three covered in an itchy, red rash all over their scalps and young bodies. Shelly was horrified and rushed them over to Doc Joe. The problem was Doc Joe was the veterinarian in town. We didn't have a human medical doctor within sixty miles. This was certainly a drawback for many little towns. Doc Joe got to the bottom of it, though, when the girls confessed their product and how it was made. With Shelly gagging all the way home, the girls all got bathed, separately this time, and the ointment from Doc Joe smeared over the reddest areas. Funny, the girls thought, it wasn't so itchy anymore. The new product was definitely a bust.

I was pretty much in hysterics hearing of Shelly's exploits with her girls, and Trish managed a few quiet laughs too. So finally, I asked her, "Trish, what's new with you?"

She began to tell of a new line of quilting material they were getting and how Mrs. Atwater would probably come in and buy it all before anyone else could get some. And then she kind of snapped! The subject changed to "this little town, with the same old people and the same old stuff going on and no one to date, let alone marry… etc., etc., etc." She really let loose and her voice got a little louder and her eyes got glassy and then…It happened!

In an effort to save poor Trish from her pity party, I started telling this big, untrue story about how this professional guy had called up the paper and asked about our town. You know, like what it was like, the size and "feel" of the town. I said I talked to him for quite a while and that I'd send him a Chamber of Commerce pamphlet. I pretended that I asked him why he was interested. He apparently "told" me that he came from a rather large city down south and was looking for a different way of life, where people cared about each other and worked together. This was coming for him at a perfect time when he could relocate his business and find the place he was thinking of.

I then went on with my big story and gave a few more details and built this rosy picture of what might be. I don't know what possessed me to say this stuff. I wasn't a liar, ever! Well, maybe a little fib when Shelly totally forgot to comb her hair after her shower and suddenly discovered it moments before the big meeting of the PTA election board. I told her she looked fine. But I don't lie, and here

I was, inventing a story that I hoped would make Trish feel more hopeful. Maybe give her something to anticipate or dream about. Oh gosh, who knows? Maybe the whole thing would just fade away. I now realized this could backfire horribly, but what could I do now? I, Miss Community News Editor, had started a *rumor!*

CHAPTER 2

It's Growing!

I hesitantly looked around the table of my unsuspecting friends to gauge their reactions to this overwhelming and exciting news, and there was genuinely a little excitement and lots of questions. What was his business? Did he sound handsome? Was he single? Did he like dogs or cats or birds? My goodness, my friends thought of weird things to ask! In my anxiety at becoming the world's biggest liar, I just couldn't stop. I kept talking about it until my lunch hour was almost over, and I had hardly eaten yet. I scarfed everything down quickly (I'd worry about heartburn later) and scooted back to my office.

I plopped down into my rolling swivel chair behind my desk and thought I had finally become truly self-aware. I am a big, exaggerating, hopelessly romantic, ever-optimistic, gigantic rumor starter! It's a total wonder the paper got published at all that day. What had happened to me? Maybe I wasn't so "mentally balanced" as I had thought earlier in the morning.

My day was far from over, even though the paper had gotten out on time. The delivery boys and girls had picked up their bundles and were distributing the issue throughout the town. It's funny how a small town can come to depend on a sixteen-page newspaper for all the latest happenings. People waited anxiously to see their newborn's scrunched-up face in the picture taken by hospital nurses with the proud parents' names below. And could it be that Marge and

Elmer Lewis had been married thirty-five years already or that the city council needed more donations if Main Street was to have new Christmas decorations?

I was sure to get a couple of calls tomorrow about how James had missed delivering to someone or Annie threw her delivery right into the bushes *again*. Try as we might, it's hard to catch every typo or get every delivery perfect every time. My job included hearing the complaints, responding without my temper flaring, and trying to fix the problems.

I arrived home to my cozy cottage at about 5:00 p.m., and my kids had gotten home at about four. Even though I was reminded by them almost every day that they were "almost adults," I still worried about what could possibly happen during that hour. Today I found them both sitting at the kitchen table with books spread out and some homework being done between bites of bananas and cheesy crackers. Except for the bananas and crackers right before dinnertime, perhaps they *were* "almost adults," taking responsibility for getting their assignments done without reminders from Mom—well, at least tonight! So hugs and kisses all around and on to phase two of my busy day.

As I started making a dinner that didn't include bananas or cheesy crackers, I still couldn't get the thought of that rumor out of my head. I tried rationalizing. I was just trying to give Trish something nice to think about. Yeah, that was a compassionate thing to do, wasn't it? And, well, maybe nobody really thought much about it, and tomorrow, they wouldn't even mention it. That was a possibility perhaps. Or *maybe* a third of the town would have heard something about it, and the other two-thirds would know by the end of the day! I think I shuddered a little at that last thought.

It was during these rushed dinnertimes that I really appreciated my Italian heritage. It was so easy to make a yummy dinner in a snap. I often tried to imitate Tony and Anna's specials but never was quite as consistent nor capable as they were. Hmmm...tonight...sausage and peppers and penne pasta with green beans sounded delish. And bonus alert, it was also nutritious! I must admit I do take a little pride in my well-balanced meal planning. Thank you, Mrs. Bartholomew, for those home economics classes; and thank you, Dad, for the Italian flare!

Throughout the evening, I kept finding my mind returning to the events at lunch. I was pretty good at convincing myself that the first scenario of everybody just forgetting about it was surely the most likely outcome.

*****

The next morning, I found myself hurrying as usual to get the kids up and going. It really wasn't very hard because, I surmised, I did have the best kids on the planet. Yes, that sounds kind of "braggy," but I truly felt that way. Daughter Tiffany, not quite seventeen, was just a jillion times more of a treasure than all the jewels in the store which shared her name. She was a beauty, very responsible, dependable, conscientious, tons of fun, determined, and smart. My son, Bryan, was handsome, a light in our home with an ear-to-ear grin that made everything seem better. Bryan was the risk-taker, and at age fifteen, it always worried me a bit. He was an excellent student like his sister and mostly got good grades without much studying. He loved to read and seemed to remember most of it. We called him the trivia king. He knew a little bit about a lot of things. The both of them were loved so much I could scarcely keep from hugging them into little balls of butter!

Anyway, this morning was like most other weekday mornings, up very early to get the kids out the door for an early morning religion class before school. Tiffany was also in student government, and some days she had a student council meeting before school. She had a nice movie star look-alike boyfriend. Bryan, on the other hand, wasn't about to spend his hard-earned money on any girl at this point. Both had part-time jobs. With me working full-time, scheduling was always a priority.

Somehow it all seemed to work out most days, and today was one of those days. I blew into my office, peeled off my warm yet snazzy short white jacket with navy blue lamb's wool lining, and tossed it toward the hook behind my desk. It caught! It was a sign!

Okay, I thought, *today is gonna be great!* After stuffing my purse into the bottom desk drawer, I set to work, opening up the office, and turning on the machinery we needed to get out another edition. Ron had actually turned on the copier today—a miracle! I began looking over the pile of typeset articles on my desk waiting to be proofed. I pretty much had forgotten all about the dreaded rumor.

Janna came wandering in a few minutes later, loaded down with advertising proof sheets for various town merchants. She had just had a quick breakfast with Jackie at the little shop near the city hall. I did the polite thing by saying, "So what's new?" Why? Why did I do that? I opened up the flood gates.

Turns out Jackie told the mayor about the new doctor looking to move to our town. Wait, who said he was a doctor? Janna said I told all the girls that at lunch yesterday. I didn't, though. I only said a professional. Jackie apparently thinks that all professionals are medical doctors. Anyway, Mr. Mayor got all excited, she said, another miracle, actually, and he quizzed Jackie about the newest soon-to-be resident. Oh gosh, the rumor was growing!

The bottom line of that whole conversation was the mayor was now intent on luring the "doctor" here and wondered how he could make the town more attractive to the handsome, young doctor, a recent graduate of a very prestigious medical school! Janna sat down at the desk opposite me and asked what I thought the town could do.

Why ask me? I don't know the doctor! Yikes, I even had a momentary lapse of reality and thought of him as real. I just shrugged it off and kept reading the latest galley of news, hoping really hard they'd all just let it go.

I had just finished looking at this week's submission of women's bowling scores when Charlie, our editor, appeared at my desk. He'd been thinking housing and office space would be what the new doctor would be looking for if he were to stay in our town. He asked what I thought of that place on the north end of Main Street. He went on to tell me that the house had been empty for some time now and was pretty rundown but had a really good entryway that could serve as a patient waiting room, and then that big front room could be the doctor's office. He could have his office at the front of the house and his home in the rooms behind. *Charlie,* I thought, *is renovating a house he doesn't own for a guy that's not real. Wow.*

Charlie wandered off to the press room and would, I hoped, just let it all slide. People will move on to other things. Surely they will, won't they? The rest of the morning was fairly uneventful. The usual phone calls came in. Customers and business owners came in to place ads or submit information for a story.

One thing that always struck me as an interesting part of a small-town newspaper was the classified ad section. We had a full page set aside in every edition for the classified ads, and surprisingly, they were always a good read. They were especially interesting to our head typesetter, Bud. He came through the front office several times a day, and he *always* stopped to rifle through the box we had set aside to collect the classifieds until they could be typeset later in the day. I'm not sure what he found so inspiring in those ads, but he'd read and laugh or smile or nod his head at each one. He liked getting the jump on a good deal.

How people used as few words as possible to make up their ads was often quite creative. I had heard the story of Betty, whose husband had died at the ripe old age of eighty-seven. Those two seemingly had a mild love-hate relationship, mostly due to his obsession with hunting, and when it came time to place an obituary in the paper, she decided to take out a classified ad instead. Our policy was any ad under ten words was free. Betty chose "George died. Rifles for sale." Short and to the point, I guess. Bud bought the rifles.

CHAPTER 3

Odd Occurrences

As I sat busily reading the soon-to-be-published articles regarding the city council's latest meeting and the announcement regarding the possible expansion of our one strip mall, I saw Arnie Reynolds across the street. *Oh please don't come in here today*, I thought and was relieved to see him entering the post office instead. I was just not in the mood for another round of discussion of bowling scores.

About then, Rudy, our sports editor, came by my desk. He was the nicest guy, thoughtful, and upbeat. He and his wife had lived in our town all their lives, and they knew everybody. One time, he became concerned that as a single mom, I had not done the proper maintenance on my car. In reality, he was exactly right. When *was* the last time I got the oil changed anyway? He asked for my keys, took my car, and had the mechanic at the gas station give it a full check-up. I tried to pay him for his thoughtful service, and he would not take my money. I always loved dear Rudy. That was a big help to me, and I will never forget it.

Anyway, he asked me if I'd seen Arnie, which seemed a little odd, and I told him I'd seen Arnie earlier across the street at the post office. Right then, the door swung open, and there stood Arnie. He was a big guy with a potbelly and a loud voice. *Oh no*, I thought, *he's gonna rain down his bowling score complaint on us*, and it was sure to be a downpour.

But surprise, surprise! They greeted each other, and Rudy threw on his jacket, and out the door they went. If I wasn't so busy, I would have stopped to think of the various scenarios that would bring these two together. It did seem just a little odd.

As I got back to reading and writing and thinking and reading some more, I casually glanced up through the large plate glass windows that ran across the front of the entire newspaper building. I caught a quick flash of Trish in sweat pants, walking pretty fast down the sidewalk. Was she exercising? Trish was *not* an exerciser. Not ever! She would actually spend a lot of time avoiding structured exercises. The girls and I often had invited her to join us for some jazzy dance class or aerobic workout at the city center, but she never would. Once she told us she couldn't because she had planned to think seriously about paint colors for her bedroom that day. That's an excuse from somebody who *really* doesn't want to exercise. Hmm…seeing her possibly exercising was the second little oddity that had happened today, and it wasn't even lunchtime yet.

Right after lunch, the "Every Blooming Thing" van pulled up to the office's front door. A most gorgeous arrangement of red roses now sat on the front counter. Two possibilities existed as to the lucky recipient. It could be JoAnn, as she sometimes got a delivery from a truly secret admirer. Or it could be from my sweetheart, Jeff, who was also the captain of our volunteer fire department. Jeff didn't actually live in town. He had a farm about ten miles west where he raised corn, wheat, hay, pumpkins, and a small herd of cattle. We had met when he came into the office to place an ad for the upcoming Harvest Festival a year ago and had dated some since. This was a big step for me since I had not dated anyone since the untimely death of my husband some four years ago. The time seemed right now, though, and certainly, Jeff was a "safe" place to start.

Being single in a small town was sometimes a challenge. Trish and I were the only "sort of younger" people I knew who were actually single. Our town was luckily filled with families and couples. We had a few older folks who had lost their true loves to old age or illness, but mostly, our town was a family town. It gave the place a very homey feel most of the time, but Trish and I sometimes felt like a third wheel. I had my kids and their activities, but Trish was truly alone. I started to wish there really would be an accomplished new doctor who would become her happy other half. The rumor was back at the forefront of my brain again. Why could I not stop thinking about it? It had gone from a baby rumor to a toddler!

Turns out the flowers were for me that day, which meant lots of teasing from my coworkers. "Are those from Captain Jeff?"

"Oh, he's got it bad!"

"Are ya gonna get married?" And many more similar comments. It was good-hearted teasing, generally. But I noticed there is one thing that married people just hate to see, and it's any single person! I can't tell you how many times someone had a cousin or an old college friend or a newly divorced son of a friend they knew in another state that would be *perfect* for me. Right now, outside an occasional date with Jeff, I thought being a mom and the community news editor was all I could handle. Oh yes, I also was a giant rumor starter. All that is enough for anybody.

That evening was especially hectic because Tiffany and her friends were getting together after dinner, and she was hurrying to get her piano practice done before the fun began. It wasn't that piano practice wasn't fun, but at least thirty minutes every day seemed like such a *long* time when you had so many other things to do. I had tried the "mother logic" on her by telling her that out of all the things she could do today, learning to play the piano was a talent that she could share with others for her whole life, perhaps, and that many people would appreciate hearing her music. The roll of the eyes and the heavy sigh let me know my attempt at "mother logic" fell on deaf ears.

Changing the subject, I asked her what they were all going to do tonight. She said they were going to decide and plan what they could do for the new doctor coming to town! What? Wait a minute! I literally felt my heart skip at least two beats, and my mouth was suddenly hanging slightly open. Containing my shock that even teenagers knew the rumor, I tried casually to ask what was she talking about. She told me Sammie's mom had told her that a medical doctor was moving his practice to our town soon, and wouldn't it be nice to figure out some kind of welcome for him?

I was trying to think how Sammie's mom could have possibly known this little tidbit. Of course! It had to be the mayor's wife who happened to be BFFs with Sammie's mom. That had to be it, and once these two heard about something like this, it would be like the wildfire we had in the mountains last spring—enormous!

Really, now really, I just could not imagine so many people spending so much time on someone or something they didn't even actually know! It was one thing to just make an offhanded remark about something like I had innocently done but a whole other thing for the entire town to pick it up and run with it like a Mountain View High School football player! I started seeing those sparkly lights in my field of vision which sometimes indicated a migraine headache coming on. *Breathe*, I said to myself. *Just breathe.*

CHAPTER 4

Batter Up!

The next morning, there was "frost on the pumpkin," as they say. It was beginning to really feel like fall. Most of the leaves were falling from the trees which I always found to be a sad event. Why couldn't they hang on one more month, for Pete's sake? We barely had time to enjoy them, and they were gone, and Bryan would not be happy that he had to rake and bag them.

I tried to get Tiffany to wear a warmer coat, another tough thing about autumn. Most kids seem to be born with the idea that wearing a coat was like a ball and chain around their neck or being forced to walk the plank. There were lots of excuses like, "It's not cold," even when the temps were below freezing. My favorite excuse from my teenagers was "I don't have room in my locker." The first time they tried this excuse, I told them that they didn't have lockers at Mountain View High School (the lack of lockers had been a hot topic at school board meetings, and I regularly read the articles that Charlie wrote each month to keep our public informed).

When that secret was out, they quickly said, "What we mean is, we have no place to *keep* our coats and we don't want to carry them around all day."

Oh, I see, teenagers have no muscles even though they can play football and lift weights and hit a baseball out of the park! Yeah, I get it.

After some stomping around and heavy sighs, Tiffany put on her coat. Bryan had already given up the protest and was out the door in his warmer coat. He seemed to sense a little more quickly than Tiff did that I was determined to win this battle. *Geez*, I thought to myself, it wasn't like I was trying to force them to carry an embroidered handkerchief to wipe their noses or something. It was just a coat! I was a good mom after all, wasn't I? I was just trying to keep them comfy, warm, and free of the diseases that accompanied every kid, everywhere, in the changing weather of early winter.

Leaving the first battle of the day behind, I left for the newspaper office. My office seemed especially welcoming this morning. The cleaning crew had polished up the floors and counters, and my desk was neat and tidy. I actually always left my desk each evening organized and clean. I'm the kind of person who would hate coming into a mess like some of my coworkers did. I also could not abide getting up in the morning to a sink full of dirty dishes from the night before. Some might call me a neat freak, but I didn't really care. It was the way things needed to be so I could feel peace in my mind.

As I pushed my purse into the drawer, I glanced at the pictures I kept on my desk. My kids were really cute, I thought, and then I saw the crime of the day! I kept a small picture of Jeff there, too, and today it had a big, black mustache scribbled on it. I was determined to find the culprit that would desecrate my picture. As each member of the *Bulletin* team passed by my desk that day, I questioned each one. "Did you do this?" I would accusingly ask. Nobody fessed up. I'd need another picture.

Trish dropped in that morning just to say hi. *Unusual*, I thought. And she was slightly smiling. Trish just had that kind of face that needed an extra nudge to get a smile out. I mentioned I'd seen her power walking the other day, and she said it was time to get tuned up. I think she meant *toned* up, but whatever. "What is the motivator?" I asked her

And she said, "Nothing, really, just the right time."

"Well...okay." And with that, she was out the door. Maybe I needed a "tune-up" too!

I had quite a few announcements to go through that day. Three for upcoming weddings, several meetings for various groups, and one that about had me fall out of my swivel chair! A meeting to revitalize the old baseball field on Apple Way. That "field" was more like five empty lots that were overgrown with a falling-down fence. The time of the meeting was left off the hastily written paper, so I looked for the name of the submitter. It was Arnie. I'd just call him and get the full story and the time.

Arnie answered the phone in his usual gruff way, and he seemed surprised when I told him why I was calling. He insisted he did *not* leave the time off his announcement, so I tried another approach. Could he *confirm* the time of the meeting? Oh sure, he could do that! It was 7:00 p.m. I told him I was curious as to why he was thinking about redoing the ball field. He rather annoyingly told me the new doctor *loved* baseball, and perhaps having a good field would help him make up his mind to stay in our town. It was back! The *rumor* was back and rearing its head on Apple Way! Arnie said he and Rudy had come up with the idea over coffee a few days before. I remembered they had left the office together that day.

When Rudy came by my desk later, I asked him about the ball field. Yes, he thought it was a great idea. "The schools could use a good field, and maybe the town could get a Little League team together." He was going to ask Jim Caudy, the baseball coach at the high school, if the baseball players would like to help with the revitalizing project. Maybe they could get it done in time for spring training, or if they worked fast, maybe by the time the doctor showed up to look around.

I have to tell you I was feeling a little sick in my stomach after talking with Rudy. And it wasn't because I had forgotten to wear my coat and was coming down with something. I was feeling woozy because I couldn't fix the damage my foot had done to my big mouth, and people were really going to hate me if they did all this work for no reason at all. But that giant bowling ball of a rumor was rolling down the alley, gaining speed, and I couldn't think of any way to stop it.

CHAPTER 5

The Renewal Project

Things were really getting busy around the office with the holidays just around the corner. Merchants were already thinking of how best to entice shoppers into their stores. Holiday activities were past the planning stage and moving closer to actually happening. The weekends from November first through January first were more than half filled with everything from the Harvest Festival to the New Year's Bash. If you wanted to have things to do every day, now was the time! Ad space in our newspaper was going fast to publicize these events.

That's probably why I was surprised to get a memo from our ad department, asking me to reserve some prime space for a special addition to the paper. It got my curiosity up and decided to wander up to Janna's office and see what was up. I stopped by the soda machine and picked her up a diet cola. It was her favorite drink of all time, right behind black coffee and red wine. Janna was one of those people who liked having a mug or glass or water bottle in hand at all times.

Janna was huddled over her computer, typing away when I arrived. I handed her the soda, and she profusely thanked me as if she had been stranded in the Sahara Desert for three months with no water. When I asked what was up with the space reservation, she excitedly told me that our publisher had decided to sponsor a community-wide fundraising and ongoing service activity to spruce up, improve, and modernize our little town. It was all going to be an effort to attract the doctor!

Every time someone mentioned "the doctor," I felt my chest tighten up a bit, and my eyes would open a little wider, and I would feel just a little sick. Anyone who could read body language would certainly be able to spot my signs. Today, as I walked back to my desk, I thought, *Okay, Miss Rumor Starter, just roll with it.* Since no doctor was coming, what would it hurt to clean up the town, fix a rundown house, or mow the weeds on the ball field? Weren't they all good things for us to do anyway? Maybe it was actually a good thing to start a rumor. Yeah, let's go with that today.

As I neared my office, I saw Jeff standing at the door talking with Charlie. Now my heart was skipping a few beats. I was always glad to see him. Sometimes, when I'd see his truck around town, I'd get just the slightest bit breathless…like the "vapors" I heard about women getting in the old days. Good heavens, I was no teenager, but when Jeff was around, I think I could revert a bit.

Charlie left to cover the city council meeting, and Jeff and I had a moment to chat. He did have the nicest smile. His eyes would get even more sparkly blue when he smiled, and I would get that little tinge of breathlessness. He asked if the kids and I would like to go to dinner tonight. Well, of course! A day without cooking dinner was always welcome, but a meal with my three favorite people was a super treat for me.

Our little town only had one real dinner restaurant. It was a family restaurant with wooden tables and chairs, checkered tablecloths, little lanterns in the center of most of the tables, and a menu filled with "comfort food." My kids and I came bouncing in, perhaps a little louder than we should have been. Jeff was already there, seated across the room, and gave us a wide grin and a big wave. It was so nice to be welcomed so genuinely.

We settled into the cozy corner table, and everyone was talking and smiling and laughing. This was the family life I had always dreamed of which had eluded me and the kids. I sat back and watched the easy way Jeff talked to the kids and their warm responses and easy conversation. Tiff wanted to know how his dog was doing. She loved that big, puffy white dog, and the dog loved her. Tiff was the only person who could put a scarf around that dog's neck and sunglasses on her face, and the dog sat patiently through it all. Bryan wanted to know if there had been any big fires lately and all the details. After the second visit of our waitress, we thought we should look at the menu and get down to some serious dinner options.

The ordering of food was always predictable in our family. Tiff always wanted a salad and had to be talked into eating more. Bryan always wanted variety, sometimes a burger, sometimes Mexican food, sometimes a juicy steak. His choice, most times, was a surprise to me. The predictable part was that I couldn't predict his choice—ever. Jeff would always try something new. Perhaps it would be the special or the fish of the day or the buffalo burger. Whatever he chose, it would something I had not seen him eat before. And me, I'd choose either something Italian or something Mexican or maybe the prime rib or maybe the roasted chicken with cheesy potatoes. I pretty much liked everything.

As the evening moved along, Jeff casually mentioned he had been tasked by the forest service to help mitigate some fire danger by removing quite a few trees in the canyon above our town. In an effort not to waste these beautiful pine trees, they had decided to not just cut them down but to pull them up with one of those big tree scooper machines and offer them to the city for a beautification project along our Main Street. He thought it would make the street more attractive, too, and the *doctor would like it!*

He said that so casually it almost slipped by me. I asked him what doctor he was talking about. And he relayed a *big* story about the new family practice doctor that was considering moving to our town. Oh my gosh, the doctor now had a specialty—family medicine. Jeff had talked to Charlie about the tree relocation project, who brought it up at the city council meeting, and *bam!* It was a done deal.

I asked Jeff if he would have any input into the selection of the specific trees coming to Main Street. He said he probably would, and then I asked him to get all the pretty Christmas fir trees he could. I could almost see it now—our transplanted trees aglow with sparkly lights amidst the old-fashioned streetlights with the new decorations the city fundraiser committee would be buying attached to them.

It was about then that a new idea struck me like a thunderbolt between the eyes! What if the community project the newspaper was going to sponsor was a storefront renewal project? And each block would work together to win the prize, which would be… I couldn't quite think of the prize actually right then, but I would work on it. I was getting hooked on my own rumor.

I suddenly became aware all three of my dinner companions were staring at me. I think I had been in my own little world for a moment there. "Mom? Hello? You in there?" I thought I heard something like that, and it snapped me back to my happy surroundings and our soon-to-be-devoured dinner. But in the back of my mind, I kept thinking, *A prize…a prize…what would be a fantastic prize?*

That night, I lay awake for at least twenty minutes thinking about "the prize." Twenty minutes doesn't sound like much, but for me, that was a *long* time. My head usually was in sleep mode about ten seconds before my head hit the pillow. I went to sleep that night, envisioning a welcoming Main Street, a new baseball field crowded with neighborhood families, a Main Street with wonderful shops, a fresh and professional little office on the edge of town, and a top-of-his-class family doctor greeting his new patients. And oh my gosh, I heard that the doctor had asked Trish out on a date! *I'm out of control!* I thought. *Go to sleep right now!*

CHAPTER 6

The King Size Undertaking

The next morning, around ten, the front door of the *Bulletin* flew wide open with a thud as it bounced against the wall, and there stood Mrs. Atwater. She was the female version of grouchy Arnie, an older woman with a gruff exterior and a demanding sort of way about her. If she cornered you somewhere, you might never get away, and you'd hear every complaint she had that day. For a moment, I wondered if every older person got like that. And would I someday be some town's Mrs. Atwater? I determined right there I'd *never* be that! At least I *hoped* I never would be.

When I saw Mrs. Atwater around town, I often wondered how a sweet little baby girl could grow up to be cynical, sometimes rude, and often a person others wanted to avoid. I felt a little sad for Mrs. Atwater. I knew her husband had died years ago, and her only son lived back east somewhere and seldom came to visit. There were other widows in our town, but Mrs. Atwater's gruffness seemed to hold them at arm's length. What would it take to tear down that wall she had built around herself, I wondered?

Today she wanted to put a classified ad in the paper, and our counter girl, Diana, handed her the form and pencil. Suddenly, I found myself pulled up out of my chair, obviously by some unseen force, and staggering the few steps to the counter. *Don't do it! Don't start a big conversation!* I said that to myself several times, but I didn't listen to myself! *Why* oh *why* didn't I take my own good advice? My curiosity got the best of me, that's why, and I greeted Mrs. Atwater with a welcoming smile. All it would take would be a simple "How are you, Mrs. Atwater, what are you up to this fine day?" And that could start an avalanche of complaining that could swallow you whole.

Mrs. Atwater informed me that she was putting an ad in the paper for anyone interested in making a very special and exciting new sewing project. She told me of a new line of fabrics that she had scooped up from the quilt store and how there was absolutely none left at the store. *Trish will be fuming about that for sure*, I thought.

She had selected a pattern she saw in the latest edition of *Everyday Quilting* and was thinking of using that and how everyone who worked on this special project would be making blocks from the fabric and signing their names, and it would be a momentous and sentimental gift for someone. I asked her who, although I had a sinking feeling that I already knew the answer.

With real annoyance, she started questioning me! She started off by asking why I didn't know all this. "My goodness," she said, "*everyone* knows, but of course, you are always working and don't have much of a social life, except for that fireman, of course. And teenagers, well, they take up a lot of time, don't they?"

Eventually, as her lung capacity started to fail her, she breathlessly managed to squeak out that this was for the doctor. Of course! He, being a tall man, probably had a king-size bed, so they were making the most lovely king-size quilt to give him for his new house. "What a wonderful idea," I said as I managed to get back to my desk.

I began to think how Arnie and Mrs. Atwater could make a terrific couple. They had lots in common, they were about the same age, lived in the same neighborhood, and both had grouchy tempers. Can you imagine those two together? Sparks would be flying from their side of town regularly. I could almost picture the smoke rising each day down Fourth Street. Jeff and the other volunteer firemen would be getting called out every day!

When my phone rang a few minutes later, I was surprised to hear Trish's voice on the other end. She never called me at work, but today she wanted to relay the *big* news! Mrs. Atwater had come into the quilt store and had bought up all of the new line of cotton quilt material, just as Trish had predicted! I was waiting to hear her explode about that, but instead she sounded excited. Again, my universe seemed slightly off-kilter. Why wasn't she mad about it?

Trish went on to explain about the "king-size doctor" and the welcome quilt they were all going to make in the shop. Mrs. Atwater was going to take the lead and organize a group, and it might be good for the store in lots of other ways, too, she thought. With a seldom-heard happy lilt to her voice, she said she had to go and ended with "Ta-ta!" I'm pretty sure Trish has never said "Ta-ta" in her whole life.

What in the world was happening? A few innocent, offhanded comments were made to a very small group of your best friends and a real four-alarm fire was breaking out all over town. The uncomfortable secret was knowing I was the arsonist!

CHAPTER 7

And It Begins…

As I sat at Tony and Anna's back table, nursing my Diet Dr. Pepper and my grilled panini sandwich, I started thinking how really out of control things had become concerning "the doctor." Jackie had told me this morning that as an abandoned property, the title to the house on the edge of town had been turned over to the city. The mayor and the city council could now do as they pleased with the property, so plans were proceeding to get working on the place. I thought, *I hope they make the master bedroom big enough for the king-size bed that the giant doctor is sure to need!* Really, Mrs. Atwater and some people's imaginations could be pretty wild and crazy! Not mine, of course.

I had also found out from Rudy that Jake at the hardware store had donated some fencing material for the outfield fence of the ballfield and that Jake's assistant manager had volunteered to head up building the two team dugouts. In fact, most of the hardware store employees were signing up to help. It was going to be the crowning event for the store's Christmas party to unveil the new dugouts and fence. The fact that the store employees were working together was kind of a miracle in itself as I was aware that two of Jake's employees had quite a history, and not a good one. Jake could not schedule them to work on the same shift for years, but here they were, each working on a dugout.

As I walked back to my office, I thought about Main Street and my idea for the storefront renewal project, and I thought, *Well, what would it hurt to give my brain a pleasant project to focus on a little bit? What about that prize?* Oh, my gosh, I had a sudden lightning bolt burn through my head! What if I could get our publisher to agree to a free quarter-page ad every week for a year? Valuable? Absolutely! Small businesses have to budget very carefully to keep their shops turning a profit. Advertising money can take a big bite from that budget when you are also trying to pay a good wage, some benefits, and maybe keep a small reserve for emergencies. If presented properly, I'd bet each block would jump at the chance to win a year of free ads. Would our publisher go for it? I'd need to present that idea very carefully.

Instead of stopping at my own desk, I walked right over to Janna's office. I wondered if she would think the advertising prize would be a good one. But, alas, she wasn't in her office. I started to leave her a note just as she walked in, water bottle in hand. What, no diet soda? She explained that water flushes out fat, and she was needing that help today.

As I explained my prize idea, Janna got quite excited. "What a great prize to offer!" she said. "*All* the stores would love that!" We both wondered if our publisher would love it too.

After school this day, Tiffany came happily smiling into my office. It was always so nice to see her sweet face. How did I get so lucky to have such a dear daughter? Anyway, she told me about school and the chemistry test—it was *so* hard—and that Jill and Chad had broken up and that her group of girlfriends had decided to paint the inside of the new doctor's house! "Turns out," she said, "Sammi's mom is a whiz at interior design, and she is going to supervise and choose colors and maybe even teach us a little about wallpaper and tile accents."

I had to smile because up to this point, wallpaper and tile accents had never been on Tiffany's radar as a needed skill. I was starting to see some value added by starting that rumor, and I was trying not to think about the day it would all come crashing down.

CHAPTER 8

My Pitch

As I walked the long hall back to our publisher's private office, I tried to plan the exact words that would sell him on the free ad space prize I had in mind. Our publisher, Richard, had been in the newspaper business all his life. He inherited the building and the newspaper from his father, and his eldest son now ran the day-to-day business. But Richard was definitely the boss. He, too, was a little gruff like Arnie, but his heart was golden. For example, the florist would send a dozen poinsettia plants to the office as a Christmas gift every year. I'd try to snag them right away and place them strategically in the best places of the front office to give us that festive spirit. Richard would stroll through, notice the plants, and begin to scoop them all up! "Hey, wait a minute!" Those were meant for the newspaper workers who had helped our florist have a more successful year. And there Richard was, taking them all home!

Being a little miffed about that and after a couple of years of employment there, I grumbled about it to a coworker. With obvious disgust, she informed me that I was totally mistaken! He wasn't taking them home. He was known to drive around town, through the neighborhoods, and "let the spirit guide him" to a house that might need some holiday cheer. He'd deliver the plants wherever he felt the need to stop.

I felt like a big putz for doubting this kind older man. On the other hand, he occasionally scared people a little by telling them exactly what he thought. There was never a gray area in his mind—things were right or they were wrong, and I found out Richard seemed always right about everything. I admired him greatly.

His door was open and he was at his desk, looking through an older edition of the newspaper. He welcomed me in with a nice smile, and I tried to make a little small talk. He, being the perceptive man he was, asked me why I was really in his office. And so it began. Well, I wanted our newspaper to sponsor a Storefront Renewal Contest on Main Street. I built up the idea really well, I thought. I mentioned the joy it would bring to our community to work together to make Main Street the cutest ever and how *everyone* could get involved and how we could make a special effort to match up those with a little construction or decorating skills with our businesses, and it would be fantastic, to say the least. Blah, blah, blah.

I used *way* too many words, but Richard let me go on about it, and then, in his usual direct way, agreed it sounded good. He noted that most of the buildings were just like our newspaper building—close to one hundred years old and held together with a lick and a prayer. Many showed some obvious evidence of their age. "A good project, but why would people want to participate?" he asked.

Matter-of-factly, I responded, "To win the prize, of course!"

An awkward moment passed ever so slowly. Richard always used very few words, especially compared to me. "What prize?" he asked. The pressure was on.

Pick the right words, pick the right words, I thought. "It will be a free quarter-page ad every week featuring the businesses on the winning block for one year donated by you!" I was very confidently direct and looked him straight in the eye.

Absolutely no change in his expression occurred, and then he said, "Okay" and picked up the old newspaper and started reading. I sat for a moment, and as I started to get up, he casually mentioned, "You're in charge of it."

Getting the okay was easier than I thought, but I had yet to give any brain time to *how* I'd get the shops interested or the craftsmen or women paired up with them. And of course, for these kinds of things, having time to do it right was essential. With our daily newspaper editions jumping to twenty-four pages through the entire holiday season, I'd have lots more work to do. There would be holiday promotions and all the feel-good stories, lots of photos, musical events, and community service projects to feature. And now an entire Main Street renewal project to head up. When I thought about it, I realized that I had actually just made things much harder for myself!

Since a newspaper office was most often a whirlwind of activity, I had learned to tune out the distracting noise—well, except for JoAnn's humming behind my desk on cold days. This tactic served me well most of the time, and I needed to concentrate especially today. If I could get through all the proofreading for tonight's edition early enough, I could spend a little time on how I was going to promote the contest. I kept my head down and my blue editing pen checking and marking for three straight hours with no breaks. When I finally looked up at the big clock, I was a bit shocked that three hours had gone by, but my desk was cleared, and I was pretty pleased with my determination to get 'er done!

After a quick stop at the ladies' room and the water fountain, I zoomed down the hall to Janna's office. Her creativity was exactly what we needed to prep a nice flyer about the contest. I explained the plan, and she was thrilled with the idea. Right away, we started scribbling what info needed to be included. The advertising exec, Dave, came by, and we piqued his interest too. "What about laying out the flyer like an ad with a holiday border, a star burst around the prize announcement, and colorful accents?" he asked.

Perhaps we could run it exactly like that in a couple of issues a week. We'd advertise for those who had skills to build or decorate or improve the "look," kind of like "idea people." They could call the newspaper office, and I'd keep a list of volunteers to share with the stores who wished to participate. Yep, the idea was coming together. My one concern was, did our little town have enough people who could or would volunteer to help? I guess we would see about that.

Janna volunteered to take the flyers around to the stores as she made her advertising visits. She regularly visited all our town's shops to ask about ads and have them approve the finished ad before publication. She loved the interaction with the people and not being tied to a desk all day. I went home this day, feeling quite accomplished and in total control. It's usually a bad idea to get too cocky about stuff like that because you never knew what would happen next week. I wasn't worried. Perhaps I should have been.

CHAPTER 9

Making Headway

Two days later, I was a little early in picking up the kids from an activity they were attending after school. I thought maybe I'd just drive around town and check out the latest happenings. On my street, most people had raked up the first leaves that were beginning to fall. It was funny, although not in a "ha-ha" kind of way, that the biggest maple tree on the street was smack-dab in the middle of the Jenkins yard. It was funny because that tree must produce about four hundred million leaves every year, and not one has ever gotten raked up by the Jenkins family.

Most of the neighbors were rather annoyed by this annual occurrence because any sort of autumn breeze at all would move the blanket of leaves right onto their property. I've seen neighbors get out their leaf blowers and blow them back into the Jenkins yard, hoping they would take the hint, but they never did. It wasn't that they were lazy exactly, maybe just not as considerate as they could have been to the other citizens on the block. I had just decided that any that got caught in the fall wind and landed in my yard could catch the next breeze which would blow them on down the road until they crumbled and just became dusty remnants of a year passing by.

I ended up driving to the edge of town on the north side, and there on Main Street was the soon-to-be "doctor's office." I was surprised that there was already a marked difference on the property. Weeds had been cut down, and a small construction trailer was sitting in front. It looked like a new roof was going on, and there was a pile of siding material lying by the trailer. The sign stuck in the ground said it all: "Coming Soon: Future Medical Office." There it was again, that sinking feeling I always got when this topic came up.

I thought I just had time to check out the proposed baseball field, and it, too, had a haircut of its weeds, and there were posts installed for a future fence. The soon-to-be infield had been graded down to the dirt, and I could easily see the diamond about to come to life. Rudy and Arnie and their gang had been busy. All for the baseball-loving doctor who would no doubt become the team medical provider.

When I picked up the kids they tumbled into the car with reckless abandon. I was always so glad to see them and hear their shouted goodbyes to friends. Ah, the carefree life of kids. Some days I wished for just an hour like that. It was a puzzlement to me, however, that they always had so much stuff with them. Every student these days had a backpack just slightly smaller than themselves but twice as heavy. What could you possibly have in those things? I went to high school and I brought books home, but I never had so many that I looked like the Hunchback of Notre Dame trying to carry them!

And what is the deal with water bottles? I knew from the water report that got published in our paper every year that we had really good water running through our pipes. Why did kids need to bring big old water bottles everywhere and sip from them every ten seconds? I know the school has fountains. How did my generation ever survive with just a few quick gulps from a fountain or a hose maybe once or twice a day? We put the first man on the moon, for Pete's sake, by barely drinking any water!

A couple of times, I asked my daughter what was all that stuff in her backpack. She would pull out the sweater that Pam had borrowed and was returning, the ever-present water bottle; a pile of papers; several books, even though she had no homework in those classes this night; hair stuff like a brush, four scrunchies, a ribbon from her ponytail from last summer; her empty lunch sack; pencils and pens; and notebooks and a planner and gym clothes! The dreaded "warmer coat" was also stuffed in there and probably had been since she got to school that very morning no matter what the temp was. I was afraid to see what was in Bryan's backpack. It might bite me or give me a disease or something.

I was grateful for these moments of "life with children," though, and wouldn't trade them for anything. It was really good to have some belly laughs and even a few shocking moments here and there. And what happened the next morning made me wish I could have stayed in those moments a lot longer.

CHAPTER 10

It's in the Mail

It turned out to be a chilly, gray morning with hints that rain was soon to fall upon our little hamlet. Most people didn't seem to like this kind of day, but not me! I liked being in my home or office with an extra light on. Somehow, it seemed kinda cozy. If I was at home, I would definitely bake something on a day like this. If I was at work, I'd feel grateful I was not a roofer or a construction guy or a concrete truck driver who had to be outside in the drizzle. Yep, my little newspaper office suited me just fine.

With the kids safely delivered to their school, I headed to the office. I walked in maybe ten minutes earlier than my normal start time, and both my phone lines were lit up and ringing. It felt like something must be happening and I had better answer. I thought it was odd that people would call our newspaper office when any perceived or real emergency was happening and ask what we knew about it. Honestly, I had not seen Mrs. Turney's cat almost get run over by that speeding out-of-state car that crashed down by Third Street fifteen minutes ago, and I did not have the police report. Nor did I know anything about Sarah Jane being rushed to the hospital to deliver her twins early. And I certainly did not know a water pipe had burst on the south side of town and how long was it going to be until it got fixed. I would try to direct their inquiries to the proper office or person and then get a little chuckle out of the absurdity of it. I was actually keeping a list of the most bizarre phone calls for any time I wanted a little humor break.

Today, though, excitement was in the air! Breathlessly, it was Trish on line one. "Really, is there a renewal project? And if so, the quilt shop is definitely in, and I'll be needing a painter's help to beautify the front of the shop. And is the prize truly a year of free ads?" The thought of a city-wide project and a terrific prize was almost more than Trish could take, it seemed.

Line two had Mary Bundt who owned the bakery on Main Street calling about the same thing. Yes, Mary Bundt was her *real* name, and she credited her name for finding her calling as a baker. Mary needed help with a tiered display table for her front window, and she needed her craftsman's name and number right away because she was getting started immediately. *Whoa,* I thought. *I have not even hung up my coat nor shoved my purse into the bottom drawer yet! Let's do things in order, people!*

I told Trish and Mary I would add their shops to the list of participants, and when I had the appropriate helper volunteer, I would give them a call. There I was, telling a little white lie *again* because I had *no* list at all—yet. What shall I call my fibbing this time? Hmmm. Diplomatic? Yes, let's call it that for now.

All morning long, my phone kept ringing. It was looking like every merchant along Main Street was after my well-thought-out prize, and making the town look great for the doctor was a worthy endeavor. I had far more shops wanting to participate than helpers calling in, but it was just the first day. When Janna came waltzing in later that morning, she seemed genuinely pleased with herself. It seems she had been delivering the flyers for the last two days like the one she casually dropped on my desk now, and the response was real excitement. My list was growing, and by afternoon, a few volunteers had called in also. I tell you that Janna was a salesperson! I asked her if anyone had resisted the idea, and she said Trish was not enthusiastic about it. What? I told her Trish was the first to call in and on the top of my list. It was hard to figure that girl out sometimes.

About then, Michael from the post office called and said they had a large bundle of mail for us today and asked if I wanted to come and get it or wait for delivery. Knowing there was always something urgent in the mail, I opted to run across Main Street and pick it up. Honestly, there was seldom anything I thought was urgent, but others in the office actually got concerned about the mail and whether it had come yet. Ron, from advertising, was one of those people. He'd buzz my office every day around 10:00 a.m. and ask if the mail was in, knowing it never came before noon. Yet he'd still make a trip to the front counter to check. One day, I asked him what was so important. What was he waiting for?

Well, it was the picture of the bicycle that was going to be on sale in the bike shop's ad, of course! He seemed annoyed that I did not know that. I guess my bicycle intuition was off that day. Anyway, when the mail did come, I saw the envelope from the bike shop, and so I buzzed Ron. "Your bike is here," I announced. He was at my desk in a flash and opened the envelope.

I glanced at the all-important bicycle picture, and it could not have been more than three inches square. Somehow the fuss about such a small thing struck my funny bone, and I burst out laughing. And then I could not stop! Perturbed at first, Ron frowned. But my genuinely loud laughter eventually had tears coming out of my eyes, and I could hardly contain myself. I had to sit down. With a voice that can carry clear across a football field, I kept laughing. People came almost running from every office to see what had happened.

Ron started to laugh. I was losing my breath now and could not get one word out about the cause of such great merriment. Before long, everyone was laughing. "What's happening?" They all wanted to know. Ron held up the picture of the bike, and of course, nobody understood the meaning of it.

One by one, they trickled back to their offices, shaking their heads but with big smiles on their faces. I finally got control and asked Ron why he didn't just walk the two blocks up Main Street and pick up the picture. He said he was too busy and turned on his heels and fled the office of the crazy laughing woman.

The bundle of mail did seem especially bulky today, and there was a box of something too. Back at the counter, I opened the box, and there was a note to me. Surprised about that, I read, "Could we please display these new pamphlets in the front office of the newspaper?" The updated pamphlets were from our Chamber of Commerce and were promoting our little town. The note continued, "We think these leaflets will encourage businesses to consider setting up shop here and hope the new doctor will do the same. Thanks so much." I replaced the old pamphlets with the new. Replacing the old with the new—that would be happening a lot around our town.

I had no words in my head for a long moment. What in the world had I done? The rumor was definitely alive and kicking and wasn't going to fade away. For the first time, maybe ever, I felt like a first-class slug. What had I done to my sweet little town?

CHAPTER 11

Guilt Can Weigh You Down

I was carrying a heavy load of guilt for not owning up to the rumor right away and for letting it spiral out of control. People were excited and working hard to make a good impression and having fun doing it. I had not told a soul that the whole thing was a big, made-up story by yours truly. It was eating at me more and more. With each new proposed project or newly thought-of plan that I heard about, I felt worse. I had to talk about it to somebody, but who?

I was mulling that over when Mr. Harriman, the band teacher from the middle school, came into the newspaper office. Mr. Harriman was a true magical wizard. He could take middle school students who could only make squeaky sounds with their instruments and turn them into a great-sounding band. He was also a bit eccentric. I remember Bryan telling me about the time he walked into the band room after school and found Mr. Harriman sitting on the top of a tall ladder, cross-legged, eating a bowl of his favorite cereal and watching a movie on the DVD player. Bryan said Mr. Harriman acted like everybody did this sort of thing and didn't even come down when Bryan walked in on this sight. In spite of his odd little habits, Mr. Harriman was well-liked by students and parents for the musicians he could unleash from their nonmusical bodies.

Mr. Harriman was looking for me and wanted to know if Tiffany and Bryan could help him with a special project. He was forming a jazz band from some of the best musicians he had worked with over the years and wondered if Tiffany could play the piano and Bryan the soulful sax. I told him I would ask them tonight and get back to him. I asked him how he got the idea for a jazz band. And it happened again! He related the story of how the new doctor had earned money through medical school by playing jazz on his trumpet with a quartet and how he would just love a jazzy welcome to our town, maybe at the opening of his new office.

Oh no! Not again! I need to stop this ballooning rumor now! My head was about to burst. Soon there would be brain matter all over my office! Mr. Harriman left, and I thought, *Who can I tell? Who can I tell?*

I settled on Jeff. He had been such a strength and comfort as I initially struggled to get settled in our town. He was even-tempered, a good listener, and nonjudgmental. He was fair and honest and could keep a confidence. Yes, Jeff was the perfect person to tell.

The rest of the day had me trying to keep up with proofreading new articles and taking phone calls about the renewal project. I wasn't focusing very well on my tasks, though, and hoped I had not made any errors on the evening edition. I did call Jeff and ask him if we could get together later and talk, and he suggested getting a bite at Tony and Anna's place after work. I think he sensed my uneasiness and asked if I was okay. I couldn't really tell him yes.

I had never been uneasy waiting to meet up with Jeff before, but this time was so different. What if he got so disappointed he just couldn't see me anymore? What if he got mad for the first time ever and threw his meatball sandwich against Anna's spotless wall? What if the kids got mad at me for messing up the nice relationship they had with Jeff? The what-ifs were endless, and then he walked through the door. He was sorry he was a little late. He had been tagging the trees in the canyon for the transplanting to Main Street, and it took him a little longer than he had planned. He saw my face and asked, "What's wrong?"

Tears just started rolling out of my eyes—no, pouring out of my eyes is a better description. I was having little body tremors, my hands were shaking, and I buried my face in my napkin. I felt his big arm come around my shoulders, and he sat there, letting me get it all out. Tony was looking over the counter at us with a very puzzled look, and I was glad no one else was in the restaurant right then.

"Oh, I have done a horrible thing!" I quietly wailed. While I'm sure he was thinking "horrible" meant like murder or shoplifting or poaching a deer out of season, he could never have guessed what I was going to tell him.

As I began my tale of woe, he just kept his arm around me and nodded his head occasionally. I saw his eyes get very wide open a couple of times. He was getting shocked by my criminal behavior, I was sure of it! Our wonderful relationship was over, I thought. How could he be with someone so devious and heinous?

I eventually finished the saga and looked up into his twinkly blue eyes. Wait a minute! He seemed to have a little smile in those eyes. Was it pity that he was feeling for such a big rumor starter? It seemed like a long time before he started having the little tremors, but instead of tears, he began to quietly laugh a little. *Okay*, I thought, *what is happening?* I was puzzled. What was so funny about my dilemma? Didn't I explain it well? *Doesn't he see the crime I had committed?* I was kind of getting a little mad, I think. *He is laughing at my pain!*

Nothing could have been farther from the truth. While he was surprised the people in our town had swallowed this tale hook, line, and sinker with no verification at all, he didn't think it was such a bad thing. Yes, I had initially misled Trish a little to perhaps give her a little hope, but the rest didn't seem to be my fault. He went on to say that small towns are just that—small enough for people to talk up a good story. Every small town probably had a story or two to tell.

I was starting to feel just a tad better, but then he went on a little more. I would, however, have to clear it up somehow. All the good things people were doing could still benefit the town, but the real reason behind it all should probably come out. The question was how and when. He said I had a good mind and a sense of caring and concern for others. He was positive I could come up with a way to quell the rumor. He said we both should think about it for a few days, and maybe the answer would come to us.

I can't tell you what a relief it was to have come clean with Jeff. Perhaps it was a little selfish to push some of my burden on him, but he seemed glad to take it on. And his confidence in me helped me gain the control I needed to find a good solution. I stopped crying and wiped the smeared black mascara off my cheeks. By the way, why does mascara come off so easily? If I wasn't allergic to the waterproof kind, today would have been a good day for using it.

Tony brought over the two Styrofoam containers of chicken alfredo I had ordered for the kids, and Jeff and I walked out, hand in hand, to spend a quiet evening together with them at my house. It had turned out a lot better than I had even hoped.

CHAPTER 12

Waiting for an Answer

Jeff's excellent suggestion of thinking about the rumor and waiting for an answer to my dilemma gave me the breathing room I was longing for. Certainly, the best way to handle this would come to me, probably at night, most likely about 3:00 a.m. That's when most good ideas come my way. I always attribute it to the theory of "first sleep" and "second sleep." It seems that years and years ago, perhaps in the 1500s or so, people regularly went to bed when it got dark. That seemed pretty reasonable because there was no electricity yet for evening lights. They would wake up around 3:00 a.m.

That first period of sleep was called the first sleep. Around 3:00, people would wake up and read or meditate or pray. That quiet time of the night was certainly conducive to deep thoughts. After an hour or so, people would fall asleep again, and this time period was called the second sleep. Since no one had bedside clocks, of course, they would designate things that happened in those time frames either of the first or second sleep. Perhaps a storm would hit during the first sleep or a fire would start in the barn during the second sleep. People kind of told time at night this way.

It all seemed very reasonable to me. I usually woke up around 3:00 a.m. to make a trip to the ladies' room. By the way, *why* is it called *ladies'* room when boys use these facilities too? The men's room is for men, and the poor littlest boys have to go with Mom to the ladies' room. Now that's food for thought! Anyway, often I'd lie awake for a while after my rendezvous with the porcelain throne. It was then that truly wonderful ideas would pop into my head. Surely, the exact right thing to do about the rumor would hit me at this time. What a relief!

It really is a wonder when a burden you are carrying is somewhat lifted. The next morning, I felt like I was walking on air. Nothing was going to spoil my optimistic attitude—no, nothing! You know you can actually choose to be happy in spite of adversity? I had heard this at church a number of times and had put it to the test enough by now to know that it worked. Today was a day for noticing the little, happy things. That brave little birdie chirping in the maple tree, the postman waving good morning to everyone, how delicious those eggs and toast looked on my plate—indeed, I was in a good mood.

Then I opened the window blinds. What had happened during my first and second sleep? There was easily a foot of "partly cloudy" in my driveway, and the snow was still coming down. The thermometer read thirty-five degrees. Why does it snow at thirty-five degrees? Shouldn't it be rain? My walking-on-air was now walking-in-snow boots! They were darling white boots with realistic faux fur trim, and that made it a little better. It was going to be a little more work than I thought to keep my good mood going.

After rolling the kids out of bed and donning the warm coats and gloves, the three of us went out to shovel the driveway and sidewalk. We had to hurry to make a path before it was time to go to school and work, but many hands make light work, as they say. Breakfast tasted especially good after the morning workout, and we all bundled up again to start our day.

Lots of people were out shoveling and scraping windshields, and kids were trudging off to school. I was thinking how winter was really upon us now and how lucky we were to only get one or two of these snowy storms each winter. Bad weather might put a crimp in our town's renovation plans. Luckily, for our town, the sun came bursting out about 11:00 a.m., and most of the snow was little trickles of water in the gutters by three. Let the renovations and improvements begin! It was going to be a good day after all.

At the office, I decided to try to match up volunteers with our various merchants who were looking for help in renovating their store fronts. I thought I'd call the stores, give them the names and phone numbers of their helpers, and let them loose to figure out how best to make improvements. Already, Jeff's thirty-six trees were scheduled to be set in place. Jeff told me that his crew did an excellent job of picking good, healthy trees.

We were just so fortunate to have nice setbacks from the street to the front of our business district storefronts. It was probably about twenty feet from the curb to a storefront, which left a wide six-foot sidewalk and room for our trees. I myself was interested to see what ideas people could come up with. As I made my phone calls, it seemed people were really looking forward to laying the smack down on their projects. "Laying the smack"—now there's an intriguing saying. Who thought that up? And what is *smack*? Another mental puzzle to solve much later.

Most people seemed pleased to have a helper or two, but I was taken aback a little at a few people's responses. When Andrea from the Kitchen Corner balked at having Jack Johnson help her construct a new sign, I wondered if there had been some unpleasant history between the two. And when Debbie from our Main Street lawyer's office seemed hesitant to have Josie help improve the curb appeal of her rather bland business, I wondered why. So I did what every good journalist would do—snoop around for the *real* story!

I called Jack first. When I told him Andrea and the Kitchen Corner were his coworkers for the business renewal project, he was quiet for just a moment longer than anyone who wasn't snooping would notice. "Fine, fine," he said.

I'm not one to "beat around the bush (another saying I could think about later)," so I just out and out asked him. Was there a reason he might feel uncomfortable with this particular job?

With just a little hesitation, he said he and Andrea had dated very briefly in college, and the end of that was "messy." Since then, they had both gotten married, had children, and were very happy, but he had always regretted that they both still felt awkward about it. Aha—message received. He didn't want to back out. I thought but didn't say that maybe it would be an opportunity to heal an old wound. I guess we would see.

With my first snoop under my belt, I felt ready for another. I called Josie. Josie was a bubbly, well-liked, busy wife and mother of two little boys. She was one of those people always willing to lend a helping hand. I told her about helping Debbie make her offices more appealing, and she squealed with delight. She would *love* to help Debbie. Hmmm, that made me think the story was at the other end of this relationship. Should I call Debbie? Well, why not? A first-class snooper would not let this stone go unturned.

Debbie was—how shall I say—a very reserved, almost somber person. She was all about business, and I suspect she was an excellent attorney and very thorough. She answered her own phone this day, and again I sensed a slight hesitation when I mentioned Debbie's name. "Would Josie be okay with you? Or would you prefer another helper?" I asked.

She thought Josie would be "acceptable." I pressed a little more and sensed she felt a little overwhelmed by Josie's jovial nature. That's the way it is for a lot of people who come off as superfriendly or very optimistic. Other people get a little shocked by it all and wonder if anyone can really be *that* happy all the time. Maybe a little of Josie's sunshine would rub off on Debbie.

It all worked out pretty well, I thought, that the businesses who wanted a little help got some, and the ones who didn't need helpers were pulling their workers together to be part of the effort. Seemed like a win-win all the way around. Certainly, time would tell.

CHAPTER 13

Little Miracles

Why do lots of little things happen when you seem to be the busiest with much bigger things? I've thought about that quite a bit over the last few years and have come up with this explanation. I think most people are actually really capable of handling one or two big chores at a time, but if a few small irritants are thrown in there also, we can really start to feel overwhelmed. *But* I've learned if we can handle *all* the problems, big and small, we feel like we have really accomplished something! So it's actually a good thing to have lots on your plate, right? We have that famed "growing experience" that is supposed to make us better humans. At the time the loaded plate is in front of you, almost nobody wants that growing experience. Not me, anyway, and not today.

I mention all that because right smack dab in the middle of really getting our renewal project workers teamed up and the ball rolling, I remembered I had not stopped at Jake's hardware store on my way to work for the front porch light bulb that had burned out. Such a little thing, but the irritation I felt at having to get the bulb before the sun went down made me frown and give everyone passing my desk the "stink eye." *It is hard to be a single mother*, I thought. I had no one to share these kinds of mundane chores with, and my anxiety about living on a darker street without a porchlight made me nervous. It was a safety thing, and I was the first and only line of defense to protect my children!

Now that thought actually made me laugh a little. Bryan was much taller than I was, and Tiffany's nickname since toddler time was "Tiffy the Tuffy." They probably could handle any threats better than I could. And our town seemed to be a super safe place. The biggest crime was most likely a parking ticket, an illegal firework, or kids speeding down Main Street on Friday night. But still, it was the idea of it all, so I took my break, grabbed my purse, and set off for Jake's.

When I pulled into the parking lot, I saw quite a commotion going on. Several guys and a couple of girls were manhandling a large wooden structure. A few people were hammering it, and a few stood by with paint cans and brushes at the ready. Sitting in two foldable camp chairs were Jake's two employees who did not get along, and they were laughing and having a soda together. What was happening? Was I in that alternate universe again? I needed to find out.

As it turned out, the guys with hammers were putting the last nails into a scoreboard for the baseball field, and the painters were just about to give the board its finishing touches. Jake's employees were "supervising" and would then haul it in the big delivery truck over to the field and put it up. It was a professional-looking scoreboard, I thought—nine innings and everything!

I made that very comment to the crew, and they all beamed with pride at their accomplishment. And then this thought hit me! Oh gosh, when those "idea thoughts" start coming, I'm like a runaway train sometimes. I mentioned how they had finished the dugout benches that had actual shade roofs and now the scoreboard. Would they be interested in one more improvement for the field? Their eyes widened just a little. Well, what if I could get Mary Bundt from the bakery to take over a little refreshment stand at the field for the high school games? Could they build her a little Snack Shack?

Suddenly, the ideas were flying back and forth, and there was noisy enthusiasm. These people actually liked doing this, it seemed. I told them, "Whoa, slow down! I haven't asked Mary yet." But as I drove away, I saw them sketching something on a piece of cardboard. *Why don't I stay quiet?* I wondered. *And* I forgot to buy the light bulb.

Since I had not taken the time to get the light bulb, I had a few minutes left to stop by the bakery. Mary was there in her pink and white ruffled apron which had at least a quarter cup of flour clinging to it. The smell was heavenly in Mary's shop and her smile contagious. We hugged, and I willingly took one-eighth of a cup of flour from her onto my new black jeans. It was a small price to pay for such warmth. I pitched my idea about the Snack Shack.

Mary tilted her head to one side and kinda stared right through me. I couldn't tell if she was about to blow or what! She looked intently right into my eyes, and for a moment, the world seemed to stand still. And then she let loose! "Yes! Yes! That's a marvelous idea! My granddaughter is seventeen, and perhaps she will run it for me, and I can split the money with her for her college fund!"

Mary started stroking her chin and looking into her display case and pointing at this and that and mumbling about what else they could carry in Mary Bundt's Snack Shack. Then she spun around and said, "We could call it 'The Bunt Snack Shack!' Bunt, bunt! Like when you bunt the ball! Get it?"

Why, yes, I did! It was a clever little twist. So we started naming some of her mouthwatering confections. *How about the Home Run Cinnamon Bun? Or her square cream cheese brownie could be First Base.* The possibilities were endless! I had to hurry to get back to work. My break was almost up!

I planned to get Mary's go-ahead tomorrow after she talked with her granddaughter, and then I'd call Jake's and pass on the hopefully good news. It had turned into a satisfying day after all, and the crowning event was when Jeff stopped by with a bulb for the porch light. Apparently, he had driven by that morning on his way to pick up a coworker for an early meeting, and since it was still pretty dark, he had noticed the burned-out bulb. He said, "It's a safety thing, you know."

CHAPTER 14

Benefits for All

The evening went by pretty quickly as the kids had some homework and then a practice with Mr. Harriman for the jazz band he was forming. Tiff and Bryan seemed rather excited about the whole jazz band idea. Since it wasn't a school-sponsored club or group, the band was not limited to being an "after-school" organization or even associated with the school at all. They could actually be contracted for small jobs and earn a little extra cash. They could play for a city event or a private party, perhaps. My kids thought this could turn into something good.

Tiffany told me that several other kids with musical abilities had asked Mr. Harriman if they could audition for the band. Even that one boy, Micah Turnipseed, wanted to audition. Micah had always been a little different, you know. For example, he wanted to be called just Ringo, no last name, like the drummer for the Beatles of my day or Elvis. He had long, messy hair, wore a really ragged denim jacket every day, even in the summer, and said things like "That's sick sauce!" when he liked something. He was nice enough, though, and I thought, *Well, I'd rather just be called Ringo than Turnipseed too!* Anyway, it turned out he was actually a very good drummer and a real asset to the band.

I also felt glad to have my porch all lit up, too, and I thought how nice it was of Jeff to notice and drop off the bulb to us. He was thoughtful that way. I had mentioned to him several times how he was one of those genuinely kind people, much kinder than I could ever hope to be! He would protest that profusely, but it was true. I had to remember to be kind. It came naturally to Jeff. All three of us were so lucky to have him in our lives.

About midmorning the next day, I gave Mary a quick call to confirm the idea of a snack shack, and wowzers! She was all about it. Her granddaughter, Brooklyn, had jumped at the idea. Mary had been researching the cost of a popcorn machine and looking at a candy bar line she might also carry. She wanted to paint her bake-shop logo on the snack shack so everyone would know where the deliciousness was made. I gave her phone number to my hardware store builder buddies, and they were off to the races.

Debbie, our resident attorney, came into our office around noon. She was there to drop off a legal notice she needed printed in the paper. But instead of being all business, she stopped to talk to Diana and even waved to me! After leaving her notice with Diana, she came by my desk. She was full of thanks for matching her with Josie for the renewal project. It seems Josie had really taken Debbie into her heart and home. Debbie mentioned how she had dinner with Josie and her family several times, and their plans for her legal office were really coming along. Debbie had even babysat for Josie once! Now that was a real miracle. Everyone thought they knew that Debbie didn't care much for children. Just shows you that when we really take the time to get to know someone, they can surprise us!

I had brought a half sandwich for lunch this day and thought it was a rather nice day for a lunchtime walk while I ate. I bundled up in my off-white suede-feeling parka, the one with the fur—faux, of course—trimmed hood, and the cutest hot pink scarf with matching gloves. I wasn't a fashionista by any means, but I did enjoy putting together a "look" that I could enjoy each day. I decided to walk up Main Street and check on the progress of our businesses.

What I saw warmed my heart, and I don't ever want to forget the feelings I had that day. Some of the storefronts were completely done or really close to being done. There were fresh coats of paint, some new signs, displays in windows, and decorative touches that really made you want to go inside each place. Even the post office, which had never signed up for the renewal project, had two very big granite-looking pots on either side of the entrance just waiting for spring flowers to overflow from them.

Jeff's trees were so full and lovely along the roadside. Some merchants had added a boulder or two or a bench or a couple of bushes to the tree area. I could see that much thought had gone into the planning of these areas. The front windows of every store were shiny and bright. I stopped to look into the inviting window of the clock shop when Danny, the owner, happened to step out onto the sidewalk.

"Hey, hello! What do you think of my window?" he asked.

It was easy to compliment his work as the window was so pretty. He had an actual electric fireplace glowing with its realistic-looking fire, a comfortable reading chair next to it, and a tall grandfather clock standing so stately nearby. With a half wall behind the scene, it looked like the coziest place to curl up and read a good book. He even had a couple of books and a reading lamp on the small table by the chair. The window glass itself was like a picture frame painted around the edges with antique gold details and a sentiment at the bottom that read, "Come Spend Some *Time* with Us!" And below that, "Watches, Clocks, Sales and Repairs."

I told Danny it looked wonderful and so inviting, and I asked him who had done the painting of the glass. He told me that Helen and Steve Hill had a special needs son, Stevie, who was about twenty-three now and that he had wanted to participate in the town project. His dad had come up with an idea to offer a window cleaning service to the local businesses. Well, it turned out Stevie Jr. was not only a meticulous cleaner; he was quite an artist too. He had asked Danny if he could do a special project on his window. Danny loved the way it turned out and spread the word up and down Main Street that Stevie was doing some beautiful work.

Stevie's dad and Danny then got together and decided to make it into a business for Stevie. Quite a few stores wanted to enlist Stevie's help in maintaining their windows and doing some specialty painting around various holidays or events. Stevie didn't want to charge people, but the shopkeepers insisted, so Stevie said yes if they'd let him do a free cleaning every three months. The businesses agreed.

The mayor hired him to clean the windows, inside and out, at the medical office and to paint a big *Welcome* sign on the arched window above the door. Mary Bundt had hired Stevie to clean her bakery window, and he had painted lace curtains on each side of her front window that showcased her new display table with platters on every tier of the most luscious-looking delicacies of the day. Danny said that some folks in town had asked Stevie to do a window cleaning at their homes.

Steve and Steve Jr. were so enjoying working together. Who could have seen all this coming from an innocent remark made at lunch with friends some three months earlier? Why, the thought of it could just blow your mind!

CHAPTER 15

Blessings

As spring began to show its first signs, the deadline for our renewal project was now only a few days away. We had published updates in several editions of the paper, and the project seemed to be the talk of the town. Everyone had their favorite block of stores. We decided to make the announcement of the winning block a community event, complete with live music from the jazz band.

Also with spring's arrival, the baseball field was now the home of our high school's spring training for the season ahead. The field was complete with fences, dugouts, a wonderful scoreboard, and the Bunt Snack Shack. Rudy had managed to obtain four sets of bleachers for free from a much larger high school up north who were building a new stadium. Our city council was so pleased with the renovation of the weedy lot they voted to change the incoming street name to Home Run Way.

Every afternoon, you could see the team practicing on their new field, and Arnie was there, giving pointers. "Keep your eye on the ball!" he'd yell to the batters. "Get in front of the ball!" he would call to the infielders trying to field a grounder. And the best thing I thought was how Arnie would pat those boys on their shoulders and tell them, "Good try! Good try! Keep at it! You'll get it!" Really, the whole thing was enough to turn anyone into a baseball fan.

Our mayor proudly had us publish a letter to the community expressing his gratitude for all the time and effort donated by our citizens to complete the new medical office. I thought if there really was any doctor coming to look for an office and home, no one could have found a more suitable situation. But now that the office was complete and had passed all the inspections necessary, people were beginning to ask more questions about who was coming, when he was coming, and even how to make an appointment! A few smart cookies in town were trying to connect the dots and find out who knew this information and what was the latest. There was some head-scratching because nobody seemed to know the details. That old guilty feeling was inching back into my head because I was the only one who knew there were *no* details.

The plan that Jeff and I made to wait for an idea to come on how best to handle the rumor was obviously taking more time than we anticipated. We often would use our secret code to check with each other. "Anything yet?" one of us would say, and so far, the answer had always been the deep, deep code word, "Nope!" Since next week was another linger-longer lunch with my gal pals, I did begin to think about telling all of them the whole story. That cloud hanging over me felt like a big bucket of dreadfulness. But, hey, I had a week to figure it out, and maybe the answer would come at the very last minute.

It was hard, though, not to see all the wonderful things that had happened because of the rumor. Finishing the medical office from a building standpoint was certainly one of them, but there were several other stories in that project. Sammi's mother had taught several of our teen girls, including my daughter, how to paint and hang a little wallpaper and even install some decorative tile. These were skills those girls could use in their own home someday.

This same sweet woman had made it a personal task to find a few specific pieces of gently used secondhand furniture that would help the doctor visualize the use of the office and home. She even found out that the Nickelsons had decided to get a more energy-efficient furnace, and their older one still had life in it so she secured it to replace the medical building's older furnace. The Nickelsons gladly donated it. Now *that* was a little miracle, right?

Another little pleasant turn of events was between Andrea at the Kitchen Corner and her former boyfriend, Jack Johnson. By working together on the Kitchen Corner storefront, both of their families had really gotten into it, and they had become fast friends. Now Jack and Andrea's husband go target shooting together, and there have been dinners shared back and forth several times. Both sets of kids have found lots in common. Nobody feels weird about anything anymore. Friendship has won out.

Even our mayor had come out of his shell quite a bit. The guy we all thought of as "secretive" turned out to just be a little shy. The city renewal project had become a personal quest and helped him crack his introverted shell wide open. In fact, our town just won the "Best Little Town in the State" award, and Mr. Mayor had even spent some time speaking in other towns to tell them the story of how our sleepy old town has become revitalized. He actually knows the people here so much better and greets them with a quick smile. I was walking behind him in the hallway of the city offices a few days ago, and I think I heard him whistling a happy tune. He has come to represent us and our town very well.

And another neat thing that happened was at the quilt store. Trish and Mrs. Atwater had become fast friends as they had planned and worked on the king-size quilt for the tall and handsome doctor! They also found several ladies who were feeling a little lonely in their lives but now happily sat around the quilt frame in the store, sharing stories. Although the doctor's quilt was completed, they were still meeting at the store and were now working on an entry for the County Fair.

And here's one more big thing, at least in my opinion, that happened because of the rumor. Jake and his two employees who used to not get along got one more guy from the hardware store and formed a bowling team. And guess what? Wait for it! They *always* turned in the men's league bowling scores *before* the deadline! I know, that doesn't sound like a big deal, but it really is to me. I haven't had one rude call about men's bowling scores in a long time.

And even though this next thing that happened wasn't just because of the rumor, it is *big* nonetheless. Just living life, confiding in one another, helping each other, and enjoying time pass made Jeff and I realize we wanted a permanent relationship. Two weeks ago, he asked me to marry him! The kids, Jeff, and I are thrilled and ready to pull our family together and live a happy life in our amazing little town and part-time on the farm.

So all that is left to do is to judge our Main Street storefronts, award our prize, and oh yeah, that little part about clearing up the rumor. I decided, *Okay, I am just going to do it! Honesty is the best policy, they say, and if my friends love me, they will not tear me limb from limb. I'm hoping anyway.*

CHAPTER 16

Time to Fess Up

The time had finally come. I knew I had to clear up the origin of the rumor soon because I had been experiencing restless sleep for quite a while. I remember the good ol' days, prerumor days when I'd tumble into bed at night and sleep like a baby kangaroo in her mother's velvety pouch. I had not been able to do anything close to that recently.

My first plan was to tell the original lunch group all at once. That seemed pretty scary. What would their reactions be? I ran it through my mind over and over again. Jackie would get a look of horror on her face and start to huff and puff about what this might do to the mayor's personal reputation and how it could damage the entire town's new found fame as the "Best Little Town in the State." Shelly might not even notice I said anything. She quite possibly would be digging through her purse, looking for her phone to check on the girls. Trish would have a horribly hurt look of true friend betrayal all over her face. *How could she do this to me?* she would think. And Janna would laugh so loud that everyone in the restaurant would turn to look. "You're kidding! You're kidding!" would be her response. And me, I'd sink pretty low in my chair. And this scenario was the *best* one I could think of if I told them all at once.

Well, then, it seemed the only real option would be to tell just one person and see the reaction and move on to the next person, eventually. Janna was going to be "the one," I decided. Timing was now my main concern. It would have to wait until the renewal project winners were announced or it could spoil the whole happy feeling everyone was having. I'd have to carry my burden a little longer, for sure. I could then picture some quiet, undisturbed meeting place without interruption and plenty of time to explain my entire sin. Yes, this seemed like the best plan.

The following day, we announced the upcoming day of the judging and awards ceremony. I had gotten a committee of a few business owners and townspeople who did not have a storefront on Main Street to join me and be our judges. We planned to hold the event in the small park on the corner of Main and First Street. Mary Bundt was going to be selling doughnuts, and Tony and Anna were offering Italian sausage hot dogs and sodas. Even if there wasn't a big award, I'd go just for the food, and I hoped our citizens would turn out too.

Jackie told me the mayor had instructed the Parks and Rec Department to spruce up the park and make sure everything was trimmed and neat. With our newspaper being the sponsor of the whole thing, we decided to get balloons and streamers tied up to the gazebo and order first-rate trophies and ribbons. The jazz band was set to play some snazzy tunes to get things rolling.

The "judgment day" finally came, and happily, our sidewalks were full of people strolling up and down Main Street to see the improvements and make their own determination of which block was best. It was going to be tough, though, because everyone had done something, and with Jeff's trees and the lovely old streetlamps, it was nearly a picture-perfect scene. The weather was pleasant enough, and as the official judging committee took our final walk up and down the street, we all felt pretty proud of our town.

At two o'clock, we gathered in the park. As the committee tallied the votes, children ran back and forth, chasing each other and screaming. Isn't it funny or annoying how children will scream even when there is no threat at all? I always wondered about that. Anyway, the votes were in. Micah gave us a long and loud drum roll, and I stood on the top step of the gazebo and announced the winning block.

I hoped with all my heart that no one would be angry that they didn't win, and I was not disappointed. Everyone cheered the winners which included Mary Bundt's bakery, Trish's Quilt Shop, Daniel's Clock Shoppe, and Debbie's Law Office. The proprietors on the winning block hugged each other and jumped up and down, and then they did an amazing thing. They came up to the top step of the gazebo, and Mary announced that they would be taking the free ads in the *Bulletin* for only three months of the year. They had decided previously that if they won, they would share one-fourth of the year with each of the three top runners-up!

Holy hollering! The crowd erupted in squeals of delight and applause. Some people were crying! The kids took the opportunity to scream louder than before, even though they didn't know why. Pandemonium had broken out! Micah and the jazz band went wild. I certainly didn't see any of that coming, but it sure felt good.

What we had here was actually what a lot of small towns probably have. It was neighbors coming together, helping where needed, friendships developing, and genuine happiness for others. When you witness this most days in your town, you sometimes take it for granted, I thought, and the Main Street renewal project happened to bring out the very best in everyone who participated.

Yeah, well, wasn't that sentiment just so lofty? It wasn't gonna last because tomorrow I was setting off the biggest firework of all time! When my news spread that no doctor was coming and there never had been a doctor coming, I just might have to pack up and find another small town to live in. I just couldn't predict the outcome, and one more sleepless night didn't help at all.

*****

By morning, I was just anxious to get it over with. I had circles under my eyes, and my normally cheerful outlook had flown the coop. Even Jeff's encouraging and supportive words didn't really help when I saw him last night. The kids asked if I was feeling okay. I didn't even feel like putting together an extra cute outfit to wear. No matter what I put on, I felt like an old lady in a bathrobe with giant fuzzy slippers and a few curlers hanging off one side of my head. Yep, I guess I was a "little" down.

I managed to get to my office right on time, and when I saw Janna coming in, my stomach began to burn. She gave me a quick wave and a cheerful "Good morning" and was in her office before I could say anything. People noticed all morning how I "wasn't myself." JoAnn felt my forehead, looking for the first signs of the flu. Diana kept turning around and staring at me multiple times. I could feel her eyes burrowing into my head, which I kept down, my eyes focused on the galleys of news I was proofing. I did think I heard a few whispers like, "Did she and Jeff break up?" and "Gosh, what is wrong?" Eventually, someone must have approached Janna as she came to my desk, plopped a diet soda on it, and said, "Okay. What's going on?"

I really couldn't quite keep the tears from forming just a little bit, and Janna actually became rather concerned. I asked her if we could meet at the gazebo during our lunch hour to talk, and she readily agreed.

The morning dragged on, and it felt like five mornings. It went so slowly. She patted me on the shoulder, and about an hour later, she brought me another diet soda. Everyone else thought I was going to the bathroom so much because I was crying or something. Really, though, the soda just made me have to go!

At about eleven-thirty, Janna came up to the front desk and was pretending to go through some ad proofs while all the time stealing little glances my way. The front door opened, and without looking up, I heard an unfamiliar voice ask Janna for our latest edition. Because almost everybody who lived in town had a subscription to the paper, Janna asked him if he was new in town. He said he was, and he had read about the "Best Little Town in the State" and wanted to check it out.

I looked up and noticed he was a rather tall man, maybe in his late thirties, and very nicely dressed. He had an award-winning smile, and Janna was already telling him all about the benefits of our town. In two minutes flat, she was escorting him out the door and pointing right and left and laughing up a storm with him.

They came back in, and she said, "I'd be happy to show you around a bit. Just let me get my portfolio." As she was straightening up her papers, she casually asked him what business he was in.

He said, "I'm actually a family practice doctor with an office in the big city. I'm a little tired of city living and was thinking of relocating to a small town where I could really get to know my patients."

Janna turned slowly toward me, and her mouth hung open so far that if she had been wearing dentures, they would have completely fallen out of her mouth and smashed on the floor! I met her eyes, which were like big glowing orbs in a science fiction movie. I think mine were the same. They left the office and started up Main Street toward the sparkling new medical office building. I sat there, completely motionless and silent. The rumor wasn't a rumor anymore.

RUMOR 2

CHAPTER 1

What Now?

I could hardly wait until Janna returned from her walking tour showing the tall and interesting young doctor around town. I was still in a complete state of disbelief at how the very thing I had completely imagined had suddenly gained a real life right in front of my eyes. I thought back to the day I told my gal pals at lunch a rather wild, totally made-up story about how a professional man was thinking of moving to our little hamlet. I told myself I had done it to give my lonely friend Trish a happy thought. Maybe this "professional" was a possible future companion for her and maybe all she needed to make her smile a little was a bit of a daydream, concocted just for her.

I had no idea my remark would start an avalanche of speculation and determination by practically the whole town to lure this imaginary person into our town. He had taken on a life of his own somehow. Suddenly, he was not just a professional man, but he was a *doctor*, who had graduated from a prestigious medical school, and who was looking to set up a practice in a wonderful little place that really needed him. He became a guy who loved baseball and music. Even his physical qualities became a topic of conversation. He was definitely tall, quite handsome, and even had a specialty—family medicine.

As the rumor spread, more and more citizens found the most creative ways to make him just love our town and everyone in it. I, on the other hand, had a runaway rumor train on my hands and could not think of any way to slam on the brakes. It had made for sleepless nights and guilty feelings, and just as I was ready to spill the beans that no doctor was coming and that I had made up the whole thing, he showed up! Yes, right in my office, only moments before I was going to tell my best friend, Janna, the whole story. What are the chances of *that* happening? And that's why I was so nervous, jittery, excited, and nearly breathless, waiting for Janna to come back and tell me all the details.

I couldn't really stay seated at my desk. I found myself pacing back and forth, opening the front door, peering down the street, walking all the way to the back of the building and the press room, and gazing at the giant rollers strategically placing colors of ink in all the right places for our newspaper's evening edition. Then it was back to the front office and another look down the street. Where were they anyway? Our town was small. Main Street was only a few blocks long. I thought maybe I should proofread a couple of articles for tomorrow's paper and just sit down. And wow, that was hard to do. I could not concentrate at all, but I tried.

After reading the same words about the upcoming Spring Concert at the high school for the third time, the door flew open, and in waltzed Janna, grinning from ear to ear. "He is amazing!" she said to no one and started to drift past my desk.

"Hold on there! I need details and I need them right now!"

Since it was a little past my lunch break, I decided we needed a smoothie to carry us through the afternoon, and I grabbed Janna's arm and pretty much pulled her right out the door. She didn't protest, and I think she was enjoying my excitement and inquisition just a smidge too much. Finally, after securing our drinks, she started to give up the scoop she had just obtained.

The "professional" had a name—Dr. Steven Schott!

I punched Janna in the arm. "No doctor has a name like Dr. Schott!"

It was true, she said, and we both would have spent more time on that info, but all the other tidbits about her walk about town were aching to be told. And the day's saga began.

They had started a slow walk down Main Street, and Janna volunteered an endearing tidbit about every storefront and its owners. The bicycle shop held particular interest for the doctor as he was a competitive bike racer, and the owner of our town's shop had once raced in the Tour de France! The *only* thing the doctor loved more than biking was baseball, he said. Janna said she had slightly gasped when she heard that and decided to take a little detour up Home Run Way and show him our newly renovated baseball field. It was "a first-class field," he said, and when Janna pointed out Mary Bundt's Snack Shack, he nearly giggled with anticipation for a Home Run Cinnamon Bun.

Back onto Main Street, they ran into my number two best buddy, Jackie, whose eyes quite nearly popped out of their sockets when Janna told her that *this* tall, wonderful doctor was looking over our town to relocate his office. After some "oohing" and "aahing," they parted ways. Janna said she was sure that Jackie's phone would quickly lose battery life due to the abundance of calls she was sure to make to tell everyone. Janna overheard Jackie's first call, which was to her boss, the mayor. Janna was convinced Jackie would then call everyone she had on her contacts list. Knowing Jackie, I'm surprised she didn't call 911 and have them set off the wildfire alert system.

At Danny's Clock Shop, the doctor apparently looked rather longingly at the vignette setup in the front window. "Oh, to have a big, comfortable chair to sit in with a new book to read just for pleasure," he quietly had said. Danny happened to be out sweeping the sidewalk, and when introduced, Janna said they really hit it off. The doc told Danny he liked his window and the unique frame painted around the edge.

Danny related the story of our painter, Stevie, his dad, and their new business. The doctor part of our visitor switched right on upon hearing about Stevie's disability. He said he'd really like to meet Stevie.

And on it went, Janna said, up the street, stopping outside each inviting storefront with a short intro to each shop and the reason this shop was so special to our town. Really, Janna was the perfect person to be the tour guide as she interacted with each of these businesses on an almost daily basis as our newspaper's ad manager. Eventually, they ended up at the proposed medical office building, and who was standing on the front step? Why, it was Mr. Mayor, front door key in hand. That Jackie! She really can light the fire!

Janna said the doctor's face fell just a bit as he saw the building. "So you already have a doctor in town," he said.

Janna assured him that no, we were just *anticipating* having a doctor in town. She introduced him to the mayor. The mayor, in typical politician fashion, shook his hand just a little too hard and a little too long, but eventually, the mayor turned the key in the front door and they stepped into the office.

I had not actually seen the inside of the medical office since its completion, and Janna related how Jackie and her teen helpers had done a wonderful job, painting and accenting the tired rooms. They were fresh and calming and comfortable. The mayor related that many people in our town had helped out or donated materials of some sort, and the building now passed all the city and state codes. He pointed out the future potential waiting room, reception area, and a short hall that led to small, former bedrooms that had now morphed into possible exam rooms.

The doctor seemed pleased, and the best was yet to come. The back of the house had been expertly transformed into comfortable living quarters. Janna used this opportunity to ask if he was married or had a family, and he said he was not married yet. "Well, this area will be a perfect living space for *you* then," Janna said with a wink and a smile. Jackie had done a beautiful job at coordinating repairs and updating the home and even placing a few gently used furniture pieces to help a tenant visualize using the space.

As he gazed around the living room, the doctor's eyes settled on the big recliner that sat beside the big back window. "Ah," he said, "a place to read that book." She thought she heard a tiny sigh.

"Do you think he is going to move here then?" I asked with anticipation.

Janna tilted her head and slowly, almost painfully slowly, said, "I guess we will see."

What kind of answer was that? "Janna! Tell me, what do you think? Is he seriously thinking about it?" I just had to know!

She told me there was, as she put it, "a real possibility."

Oh my gosh! I could hardly wait to get back to my office and call Jeff. He quite possibly would fall right out of his volunteer fire truck or off his tractor on the farm when he heard! Jeff was the only other person who knew the whole story of the beginnings of the rumor. He was not only my most wonderful fiancée but the best cohort a rumor starter could ever have. He had kept my confidences completely over the last few months. Janna and I hurried back to our office, and I grabbed the phone. It was a good thing it took about seven rings for Jeff to answer as it gave me some time to catch my breath.

In his most charming, easygoing way, he calmly said, "Hi, honey." He never suspected the nonstop barrage of new and crucial news regarding the previously fictitious doctor. I spilled every last morsel of info Janna had told me, and then I waited for a wild explosion of disbelief. Instead, there was silence. I thought we had gotten disconnected.

"Are you there, Jeff?"

"Yes, I'm here," he finally said.

"Well, did you hear me? We've had a real miracle occur here, and I can hardly breathe, and you just say, 'Yes, I'm here'?"

Well, it seemed he was sufficiently shocked by the news and said we needed to talk over dinner, but right now, he had a cow that got through the fence and was wandering down the dirt road, and he needed to go round her up. And with that, he was gone.

Well, how anticlimactic could a juicy story get, I thought! I'm having heart palpitations, and he is thinking about catching the cow. That, I guess, is just the difference between a newspaper woman and a rancher. I can spin up into the ceiling over the details of a good article, and he can lean back, chew a piece of long prairie grass, and say, "Yep." Marriage was going to be interesting indeed.

CHAPTER 2

Time to Fess Up

I had gotten home only minutes before my two high school kids, Tiffany and Bryan. They came tumbling in, loaded down as usual with big sports bags, a backpack full of heavy books, and their clanking metal water bottles. They were stirred up about something for sure and took no time at all to tell me that the doctor had come to town! I could not believe my ears! *For goodness sake, schoolchildren know all about this in only one day?* I thought. The big difference was in the details of their story.

Tiffany said he was the most handsome doctor ever, so intelligent that he had become a brain surgeon and was actively looking for a beautiful and talented wife. Bryan mentioned he had played professional baseball for a few years but had to give it up when he could not risk injuring his hands that performed such delicate surgeries.

"Whoa there, kiddos." Where did they hear such crazy details about a guy they had never seen or met? Before I could question them further, Jeff pulled into the driveway. Apparently, the cow problem was now solved, and he hurried toward the front door.

"Is it true? Has a doctor *really* come to town looking to relocate perhaps?"

Indeed it was true, and we all sat down around the kitchen table to share the information we had. I, of course, had the most accurate info, and Jeff just kept shaking his head in wonder, and his eyes were bright and open wide. *He is really a cutie,* I thought.

The kids eventually had all the talking they could stand for now and grabbed up their books and fled to their rooms to start the evening's homework. Jeff waited until he heard their doors close and he could count on them not hearing the next part of our conversation. He wanted to know what I was going to do next. What did he mean by that? There was nothing to do. A professional man had come and was looking over our town. The rumor was now a true fact. I didn't think I had anything left to do about it. Jeff felt otherwise.

In the tactful and kind way that he always spoke, he said he thought I should still come clean to my friends. He felt I had made up an "untruth," as he called it, and that I should confess to my friends.

"But, but, but," I stammered. *What would be the point of that? The whole thing had worked out just fine*, I thought. I had to admit he had a point, however. If I told my buddies the whole story, my conscience would be clear. Hopefully, it would not ruin our friendships.

It just turned out that the following day was the second Wednesday of the month. It was always the second Wednesday when our lunch group got together and met at Tony and Anna's place. The fourth Wednesday lunch was always at the Golden Girdle. We had a real schedule to keep, and they were enjoyable times we all looked forward to. Not so much this week. Jeff convinced me there was no reason to delay telling my friends how the rumor had gotten started, and I agreed. I was a little bit nervous but, well, it just had to be done.

The next morning was unusually busy. I think four or five people either called or came into the newspaper office, wanting news of the good doctor's visit. Now that his name was known, one person said he was going to check his credentials on the computer. Another wanted to know the first day they could make an appointment. And Trish came in. I almost didn't recognize her as she had gotten a new haircut and actually had make-up on! It wasn't a "first" for her to wear make-up, but on normal weekdays, she seldom did. I just had to mention her new look, and she was genuinely smiling at my compliment. She told me she had also lost ten pounds, and for a moment, I was just a tad jealous of that little fact!

Before I knew it, it was just about time to start up the street for our lunch date. I checked my hair in the ladies' room mirror and stood looking at my face for much longer than usual. "Well," I thought, "today is the day." It could be good or it could be bad. Maybe I'd still have friends, maybe not. Maybe a new rumor would start that the newspaper employed a dishonest and creepy employee who had pulled a giant hoax on the whole town. It probably wouldn't take our good citizens long to figure out who was the culprit. By now, I just wanted to get it over with and unburden my soul!

All of us got to Tony and Anna's place at nearly the same moment. There were hugs and laughter and the most delicious Italian aromas wafting through the air. We had barely sat down when Anna brought a tray of our usual soda drinks and a basket of garlic bread sticks, fresh from the oven. Of course, the most immediate conversation topic was none other than Dr. Schott.

Janna commented that he was "dreamy." Jackie said the mayor had been impressed. Shelly mentioned all her girls needed vaccinations of some kind or another, and she hoped he would set up his practice quickly. Janna asked Trish if her new hairstyle was to impress the doctor, and she shyly looked down and turned bright red. Aha! She *had* been thinking about a romantic meeting perhaps, just like I thought she might! And then I jumped into the conversation.

"Okay, listen up!" I said. The table became quiet, and I thought, *Hmm, I am kinda powerful!* Gosh, I sure could distract myself. Anyway, I then started my confession. "Remember the first day I told you all that a professional man was thinking of relocating here?" They all nodded. "Well, that was all a big fib. I never had talked to anyone on the phone about such a thing and I didn't send this made-up guy a Chamber of Commerce brochure. It was a completely made-up story to add some excitement to our lives." The table was silent for what seemed like a long time. "Did you hear me?" I asked.

I looked at their blank faces, and then quite spontaneously, gigantic loud laughter burst forth, and Janna slapped me on the back and said, "Good one!"

I couldn't believe it. Not one of them believed me. I kept insisting that no, this was the truth, and they kept laughing, and Janna kept slapping my back, and I was getting sort of annoyed by the whole thing! I could not convince them. They started shooting questions at me like how, then, did I know he was a doctor, and I said that I had never told them he was a doctor, and they, in unison, said I certainly had said he was a doctor. They kept at it. How did I know he loved baseball then? They wanted to know.

"I *never* said he liked baseball."

They insisted I did. Finally, after tiring of admitting that I was just a big rumor starter and beginning to get sore from Janna slapping my back, I just gave up. If Dr. Schott had never shown up, they might have believed my story, but his appearance proved that it had always been the truth in their minds. As our yummy panini sandwiches arrived, I thought again that a miracle must have occurred, and I was certainly grateful. We really might be getting a doctor, and I still had my friends. I was feeling blessed.

CHAPTER 3

Man Stealer?

The next few weeks had me thinking about wedding plans. Jeff and I had set the date for the weekend of July 4. That was a special time for us as we had originally been introduced by Jackie at a Fourth of July picnic two years before. We didn't start dating then, but we became, how should I say, *aware* of each other. Looking back, I was probably not a "good catch" back then. I was determined not to get into a relationship or anything that even looked like a relationship. And Jeff was all about building up his farm and fighting the occasional fire that occurred in our valley. The kids kept me busy, and my job as community news editor took up all my time, except for my sleep time which I protected like a mother bear.

It was funny I noticed that as I had gotten older, I seemed to dwell more on the thought of getting more or better-quality sleep. *Why was that?* I wondered. It seemed I definitely *needed* more sleep, but logically thinking, did I *really* need more sleep? I mostly got a full eight hours, the recommended amount by the American Medical Association. They should know, shouldn't they? I often had this puzzle rattle around in my mind and had yet to come up with a suitable answer. I was lately thinking nine hours of sleep would be so much better and seldom got that. Maybe it was the mattress. Perhaps a new one would help and would prove the answer to my sleep conundrum. I thought I should remind myself to stop by the furniture store later and check that out.

I began to focus on the wedding. Certainly, time was getting short to plan one if we were to make our date in July. How hard could it be? Get a dress, get a license, and get married. The details didn't seem like a big deal, but suddenly it became a very big deal to everyone in town.

It was probably my fault, but I thought an engagement announcement in our "Around Town" section of the paper would be a good idea. While Jeff was not one to ever want to be the center of attention, he seemed okay with it. We had a cute picture taken by our newspaper photo guy who also doubled as a sports column writer, and I whipped up a couple of paragraphs about our impending nuptials. I had written dozens of these, and in a few minutes, I was done. I sent it over to typesetting. One announcement done, check!

The announcement came out the next day, along with two baby announcements, an upcoming charity bazaar article, a picture display of Miss Wendy's latest piano recital for her students, and a report of the city council's latest plans. The page looked good and well-balanced, and our picture turned out well. No problem, right? The next morning told another tale.

I had not been in the office the next day for ten minutes when the door opened, and in walked a woman I had seen here and there but was not really familiar with. She was really tall and towered over my nearly five-foot-four frame. She was, how shall I say, a large-boned woman. She said she just had to see the woman who had stolen her man!

I looked around the office to see who she was talking about and then realized she meant me! She lit into me, right there in my office. She was obviously upset that very tall Jeff was going to marry a short woman and asked why that always happened. Tall girls always got left out, and short girls should save the tall guys for people like her. She was really yelling at me, and several people came from other offices to see what in the world was going on. Janna came in the front door right in the middle of the tirade.

Just as quickly as this woman had come, she was out the door and taking rather large steps down the sidewalk to her car. What in the world had just happened? I turned to Janna, and both of us were wide-eyed. Janna told me that gal was an elementary school teacher in the small town to the north of us, and she had seen her at the county teacher appreciation luncheon several months ago. Janna was there to give out awards from merchants in the county.

Wow! I wondered if I should take her seriously. Janna didn't think so. But who would make a trip to another town if it wasn't serious at least to her? I think I better have a talk with Jeff. He had never mentioned dating anyone really and certainly didn't feel like he was anyone else's man. Everyone filtered back to their offices, and I got back to work too. I must admit it did unnerve me just a bit. I don't think I had ever been yelled at in such a threatening manner, well, except about not regularly printing the men's bowling scores. Maybe my determination to not get into a serious relationship had not been a bad idea.

I was anxious for the day to come to a close, and it seemed that time dragged on and on. It was an ordinary day, except for that early morning explosion. During a few slower work day moments, thoughts crept into my mind, wondering if that woman was actually unhinged or if she was dangerous or perhaps in the beginning stages of some mental decline. I definitely wanted to know more.

After today's edition was "put to bed," a newspaper term for having the day's edition completely done, I found myself clocking out a little early and driving out to Jeff's farm. It was such a pretty ten-mile drive. There were a couple of pastures with mama cows and their calves grazing slowly and peacefully and a couple of wheat fields that looked like waves of light green long grasses. Before the kids and I moved here, I had thought that wheat grew tall like corn and was actually surprised to see it only grew about eighteen to twenty-four inches tall. In another month, it would turn from light green to a more golden color and then be ready to harvest.

Some of this grain could become the soft pastry flour Mary Bundt used in her delicious baking recipes. I arrived at Jeff's farm feeling much more relaxed than when I had left my office.

Jeff greeted me with a big hug and a sweet kiss, and we walked up to his big front porch and sat down in the two rocking chairs that overlooked the fields beyond. After a few simple exchanges of daily topics, I began the conversation I really came to have.

I told him I had a very unusual visitor first thing in the morning. His face registered genuine shock when I gave him the details. I saw so many emotions on his face. At first, he seemed confused and puzzled, then disbelieving, then a bit angry. Not angry at me but angry that this situation had happened to me. He then went on to relate the details I did not know.

About two years ago, he had gone to the tractor show in the big city south of our town. One of the salesmen for a well-known brand of tractors turned out to be a classmate from the agriculture college they had both attended. They laughed and joked around and looked at all the equipment for quite a while. This salesman then mentioned his cousin was a school teacher just north of Jeff's town, and hey, wouldn't it be fun to get his wife, his cousin, and themselves together for dinner or something?

Jeff agreed and didn't think much about it until his tractor buddy actually called a few weeks later. And of course, the cousin turned out to be the woman who had come to my office this very morning.

Jeff went on to say they had had a nice dinner, but the cousin had made him feel a little uncomfortable. She was "kinda pushy" and a little overly friendly, and Jeff said he was glad when the evening was over. He said he and I had just met, and even though he had not called me yet for a date, he had been thinking a bit about doing that. This girl didn't interest him at all, he said, and he had not seen her since. He thought it was weird that she even remembered him and strange that she would do what she did this morning.

We then went on to speculate on what would happen next. Probably nothing was the first idea, and the last idea was she would become my stalker. We laughed and decided to just forget about it. Maybe we should have thought about it just a bit more seriously, but the evening was so beautiful, the songbirds were calling to each other, and life seemed pretty peaceful on that porch. Little did we know that this wasn't going to last.

CHAPTER 4

The Break-In

It was only a week later when I received a frantic cell phone call from Tiffany. She and Bryan had just gotten home from school only to find the back door standing somewhat ajar and all kinds of things strewn about the house. She said she had called the police and then me. I retrieved my purse from the bottom desk drawer and ran for the door.

"Stay outside until the police get there," I told her. "Don't touch anything!"

My coworkers were looking worried and concerned as I bolted out the door.

In those short few minutes, a million thoughts had raced through my mind. What if Tiffany had been home alone or Bryan had walked in on a burglar who had a gun? What if a thief was still in the house somewhere? I was relieved to see the police car with flashing lights in my driveway as I turned the corner.

The kids were out in the front yard, and two policemen were talking to them. They were all laughing! *This is no laughing matter*, I thought. *What's wrong with them?* I think I was getting a little "hot under the collar" and laughed for a second myself when I noticed I had on a V-neck collarless shirt. I pulled up in front of the house and jumped from my car.

I heard Bryan tell the police I was their mom and I hugged them both so tightly that they protested a little. "We are fine," they said.

"Fine? You're fine? Well, I'm not fine! We've had a break-in, and I don't feel fine at all!" I looked to the police for an explanation.

Bryan jumped right in and said, yes, we'd had a break-in with a rather large furry-faced burglar who made a mess of everything. They all laughed.

Looking completely puzzled, I asked if the police had caught him. "Almost," Tiff said, "but they let him run into the woods behind the house."

"What! You let him go? He is a criminal! He should be put in jail!" I said rather loudly.

The policeman told me the jail could not possibly accommodate this guy and that he was really big and kind of mean.

"That's exactly the kind of guy you are *supposed* to catch! You are the police and you are sworn to protect us!" I stammered.

They were all really laughing now, and I was feeling like I had crossed into another dimension or something. *What in the world is wrong with these people?*

The police sergeant took over. "Okay, enough joking, you guys." He turned to me. "Apparently, the door was not securely closed when you all left this morning, and a hungry, unusually large raccoon had pushed open the door. He was still in there when we arrived, and I guess the sirens scared him a bit, and we all saw him run out the door and into the woods. He left you quite a mess. I'd get that door lock checked. It seems to stick a bit."

What a relief, although the humor in it had escaped me. We thanked the police for coming and had a couple of laughs together. We went into the house to survey the damage. "Quite a mess" was an understatement, but since the kids had found it all so humorous, I made sure they got a more than ample chance to help clean it up. As we started picking up and wiping up and vacuuming, I asked the kids if they noticed anything was missing. They did not, and neither did I at first.

Jeff just happened to drop by, and after relating the "furry-faced bandit" story to him, he jumped right in and started to help clean up. He pulled out the carpet cleaner and had the living room carpet all beautiful in short order. Finally, we were done, and I fell onto the couch, quite worn out from the excitement and the worry. As I looked across the living room and into the kitchen area, I noticed my extra set of car keys was not hanging on the hook near the breakfast table. I asked if anyone had found them, and nobody had.

"They'll turn up," Jeff said. As Jeff took a look at the back door lock and adjusted it a little, I pondered the missing keys. I thought the hook they usually hung on was a little too high for a raccoon. Maybe he was on the counter and leaned way over to get them. I thought I had remembered that raccoons liked shiny things. I made a note to myself that tomorrow I would check in the backyard and look for them. If the raccoon had taken them, maybe he dropped them in his effort to scurry away. I was too tired to worry about that now. Jeff went to pick up some hamburgers for us, and before we knew it, we all felt tired enough to hit the hay earlier than usual.

I thought I would fall asleep really quickly, but I lay there for quite a while, thinking about the keys. What if someone found the keys and stole my car in the night? As irrational as that sounds, a tired mind can imagine all kinds of things. Was my name on the key ring? Or my address? Around 3:00 a.m., I found myself with my flashlight, slowly walking around in my backyard, hoping to find the keys. No luck.

It was a good thing the next day was Saturday so we all could sleep in a little. After breakfast, I sent the kids looking around the house and yard and into the woods on a kind of scavenger hunt for my extra keys. I went to the grocery store for this week's needed items. I was walking the aisles, thinking about the upcoming high school bake sale and how many bags of chocolate chips we would need when Trish came around the corner.

"Boy, am I glad to see you! I was going to call you right after I got my groceries home. Did they catch her?" she said.

Right away, I knew she was talking about my "burglar" and asked her how she found out about it. She said one of the ladies who came in for the Friday night quilt group was a neighbor of our sports editor, Rudy, who had been in the front office when Tiffany called, and he had told his wife, Rose, that I had an "incident" at my house! Good grief! Rumors could sure catch fire in our town.

I related the whole story to Trish, and we had a good chuckle over it. "Thank goodness," she said. "I thought maybe it was that woman who had come into the newspaper office, yelling at you about 'stealing her man!'"

Now how did she hear about that? Of course, Janna had told her. We laughed, but as Trish walked away, I got a little chill.

When I got home, I called Lucky Locksmith, and the owner, Kasey, came to the house and changed the locks on the doors and trunk of my car. It made me feel a little better. I put the extra set of keys into my purse with a mental note to put them into my safety deposit box at the bank. Was that overkill? Maybe, but I just had a feeling it was the right thing to do.

On my way to work the next morning, I dropped by the bank. I was going to deposit my keys, but then I thought that I just might need them during hours when the bank was closed. I decided I needed a secure hiding place that only was known to my family, and they were going to have to swear to never tell a soul. Was I getting a little paranoid about the whole thing? Maybe, but that old adage came to mind—better safe than sorry. I hurried on to my office and got busy with the news of the day and actually had forgotten about the raccoon, the mess, and the missing keys.

As I sat busily writing my next story, a Diet Pepsi can got plopped onto my desk. "Hi, Janna," I said without looking up. "Thanks for the soda."

She pulled up a chair, and I could tell she had something on her mind.

"What's up?" I asked.

Leaning in, Janna began to tell me about her morning activity. Apparently, it really bothered her that the teacher had come into our office and had given me a loud piece of her mind. Janna decided to find out more about her. "So it turns out," she said, "the woman isn't a teacher anymore. She got fired from the school district and moved out of the town where she had been teaching. And guess where she recently bought a house? Just about one mile from Jeff's farm in that old rundown big blue house near the intersection!"

I sat there, a little stunned.

CHAPTER 5

He *Is* Coming

The next few days were just ordinary days. Nothing much new or even newsworthy was happening to write an article about. I got back to my wedding planning or rather my town got back to planning my wedding. First to jump into our event plans was Anna from our Italian eatery. She was such a pleasant person that I always was glad to see her. Short and stocky with her dark hair pulled back into a tight bun, she always wore a dark-colored, small floral print dress. She seemed the ultimate *nonna* or Italian grandmother. She still had on her white apron from the restaurant. She seldom came by my office, however, so I was totally surprised to see her.

After hugs and getting my cheeks pinched by her, Anna said she had seen our engagement announcement in the paper. She then proceeded to tell me that she and Tony wanted to provide the food for our reception as a wedding gift to Jeff and me. How lovely! How generous! How helpful and kind! I accepted right away, and she assured me she would also come up with a few items that would please my "American" fiancée. Try as I did over the time that I'd known her, I could never convince Anna that I wasn't born in Italy and that only my father was Italian.

"You are Italian!" she would say. "I can feel it in my bones!"

Later that morning, Jackie came by too. Her news certainly gave me something to write about. Dr. Schott *was* coming to our town and would be here next month! She had a list of all the details and a picture of Dr. Schott for the article. I rang our editor's desk and relayed the information. He told me to, "Hold the presses!" We would need to rework the front page. A flurry of activity followed as the article was written, the picture got processed for printing, and the layout was rearranged for its inclusion. It was going to be an excellent edition after all.

Jeff came by my office too. This time, he brought with him a little bouquet of lovely daisies. It was a "just because" bouquet. No reason, really, just because. How did I get so lucky to find such a dear person later in life? This day just got better and better. Shortly after he left, my phone rang, and it was our now-famous Dr. Schott.

This phone call was a great opportunity to introduce myself and get to know the doctor a bit. Janna was right; he was friendly and seemed very approachable. I took the opportunity to invite him to have dinner with Jeff and me when he arrived in town. He readily agreed. Turns out the reason for his call was to arrange for a classified ad to advertise for a receptionist and back office medical assistant. I took down the details and the contact information and told him it would get printed tomorrow.

He started to give me his credit card information for the charges, but I told him he would get a free ad. His coming to our town and the future service he would give us all was worth way more than the ad. He was quiet for a short moment and quietly said, "I'm more convinced than ever that I'm making the right choice to move." I assured him he certainly was, and the next day, his ad appeared in the classifieds.

As I read Dr. Schott's classified ad in our next edition, I thought back to my younger days. As far back as I could remember, I wanted to be a nurse. My father would say, "No, be a doctor!" And I would protest and repeat my desire to be a nurse. That conversation repeated itself for years! After high school, I did indeed enroll in Medical Assisting School and finished first in my class. I worked for a pediatrician for a time until I married and Tiffany was soon to be born. That was the end of that career for a while. Medical assisting only whet my whistle when it came to learning medical things.

When Bryan was one and a half, I enrolled in a private practical nursing program. If a girl could have picked a harder way to get an education, going to a mentally and physically taxing nursing school with two children under five would definitely qualify. There were long clinical days and hours of lectures and homework with two kids climbing all over me. As hard as it was to manage all that, the material and experiences were fascinating to me. I loved learning every part of practical nursing and again, finished first in my graduating class. I was asked to give the class speech at graduation, and I still remembered saying that nursing was a profession worthy of our very best efforts.

When Bryan turned five, I decided to go to paramedic school and learn more about emergency medicine. While I wasn't first in the class this time, I was close, and I completed the course with a lot more valuable knowledge. I thought maybe a Flight for Life nurse was in my future. Now *that* was the craziest idea I may have ever had because I don't really like to fly, and bumping around in a helicopter was worse than a passenger plane for sure. As I thought long and hard about it, I had a feeling *not* to do that. It was a very odd feeling but I became concerned that if something happened to me, what would happen to the kids? I had no way of knowing in a few short years I would be a single parent, and thank goodness my darling children did not lose both of their parents.

So you might ask why, then, was I working at a newspaper? I had my nursing license. Well, actually, nurses weren't paid very well, particularly in rural settings. Sadly, I could make more money writing and editing stories than helping to save someone's life. Seems odd, doesn't it? People were beginning to notice this fact, though, and I had high hopes that one day, nurses would be paid a better wage. Consequently, I took the newspaper job and found out I also liked writing and laying out pages for publication. And pretty quickly, I came to love the people I worked with. Two big bonuses of the newspaper job in our town were not having to live in a big city and not having to do shift work. I wanted to be home when my children were home, and my current job fit the bill. Living in our pretty little town was also better than any city, and eventually I discovered that Jeff was here.

Still, a little part of me yearned for a medical-related job, and I wished I could apply for the back-office assistant job for Dr. Schott. But I thought there are probably more people in town with more current experience than me who would jump at the chance to get that job. I pretty much dismissed the whole idea. It did keep rattling around in the deeper recesses of my brain from time to time.

A week later, I called Dr. Schott to see if his ad had produced any results. He said he actually had several people apply for both positions, and he would be coming to town next week to interview them. I was really glad about that and asked him to meet Jeff and me for a bite at Tony and Anna's place after the interviews were over. He readily agreed.

In the meantime, I started the ever-important job of looking for the most needed wedding item—the *dress!* Tiffany and I went into the city to the big department store that had a beautiful bridal department. I had looked through some bride magazines and kind of had an idea of the style I wanted. I knew I definitely did not want a strapless gown which requires every bride who ever wore one to constantly be tugging at the bodice because it was slipping down a bit. I knew I didn't want a princess ball gown because after all, I had been married before, and it just didn't feel right to go too extreme. I didn't think Jeff would want that either. I just wanted a pretty, classy dress, maybe in an ivory color, that was feminine and yet said "lovely bride" all over it. I found one I liked that was just right, except it was a brilliant white. I wondered if I should get it. *Not today*, I decided. We went home empty-handed.

It was a really good thing I didn't buy that beautiful white dress. Turns out that Jeff's mother who lived on the East Coast had some very definite ideas about our upcoming wedding. Jeff wasn't actually very close to his family back east. He had lived in the west for many years and loved the rural and easygoing life of farming and a small town. He told me he was very different from his relatives. I had never met them. Anyway, his mother called me one evening and gave me quite an earful of what kind of etiquette we should follow. And the biggest surprise to me was her ideas for my dress. It should *never* be white; I had been married before and had children, and white was *not* appropriate.

I thought to myself, *Oh, my gosh, that's kind of old-fashioned in this day and age.* Lucky for her, I had already decided ivory was more what I wanted anyway. I decided to let her think I was taking her advice and maybe score some points with her. But either way, the brilliant white dress was *out!*

Janna told me of a bridal shop she knew about that carried really beautiful merchandise, so the first chance I got, I drove the thirty-five miles to check it out. The shop was on the edge of a small residential area. It was a quaint, country cottage. I was truly meant to find it as my GPS took me right to it! Really, that was an obvious good omen because often in rural areas, GPS is pretty worthless. Many country roads only have a number like County Road 2. It was truly meant to be also because on the mannequin in the front window was my dress! It was just as I had envisioned it. I went in, tried it on, and bought it. I also found a sweet dress for Tiffany in the pretty pale pink color I had chosen too! I was out the door in thirty minutes!

I went home feeling very satisfied that I could check another wedding item off my list. Sleep came easily that night. My plan was definitely coming together.

CHAPTER 6

Evidence Builds

The next morning seemed rather glorious too…at first. The kids seemed extra-agreeable, and breakfast went well. I put together a really cute outfit with a denim-colored shirt with puffy sleeves and a wide lace collar and good-fitting jeans and some dressy sandals. I was so glad we could dress casually at work. It was just so much comfortable. After the kids left for school out the front door, I picked up my purse and headed out the back door to the carport when I saw it. The back window of my car was shattered!

At first, I couldn't really imagine what had happened. Did someone throw a rock, and it accidentally hit my car? Did the glass just fail for some magical chemistry-related reason? I was really grabbing for straws here, any straw actually, that could explain it. I decided to drive to work and call the glass repair shop. Maybe they could fix it while I was at work.

As I stuffed my purse into my bottom desk drawer, I had already picked up the phonebook to find the car glass shop's number. My friend, Phil, ran the shop. Phil, his wife, and two teenage boys had always been ready helpers in my neighborhood. They would do things like put up my Christmas lights on the house or surprise me with colorful petunias planted in my big pot on the front door step. Phil said he could get the glass and would get it done by the end of the day.

Janna heard my conversation and hung around my desk until I hung up the phone. She had a slight look of concern on her face. "What?" I asked her. She asked me to tell her the whole story. There wasn't much to tell, really. I came out to the car, and the window was shattered, so I came to work and called Phil.

"Hmmm," she said.

"What?" I demanded.

"Well, it's just weird that you had that little run-in with that friend of Jeff's—"

"Not a friend," I reminded her.

"Yes, but what if *she* is more upset than we realize and she broke your window? And maybe a raccoon had gotten in your house, but what if she had been there first and had taken your keys, and the raccoon came in when she left the door ajar?"

My goodness, what an imagination! I laughed it off, but it did give me a little pause…for just a moment. No, that would be crazy, wouldn't it? Later that day, Jackie came in with some information on the upcoming city council meeting. At least that's *why* she said she came in, but the topic turned pretty quickly to the woman who was stalking me! *Janna! What have you done?* I thought. Here we go again. A rumor was starting, and somehow, I was at the center of it again!

After I had laid out the final pages of the day's edition, I took a moment to close my eyes and take a few deep, slow breaths. I had read that deep breathing was very healthy for you. As you take in these nice, slow deep breaths, your heart rate can slow a bit, your blood pressure can drop a little, and the red blood cells can become more oxygenated. When you have oxygen-rich blood flowing through your arteries, you feel invigorated, and who doesn't need a little more vigor? I certainly did, and on most days, I would try to squeeze a little more oxygen into myself by doing these breathing exercises. I've been told it looks kind of weird, though, when someone walks by and I am at my desk, eyes closed, and breathing deeply. It's my "thing," as we used to say. It's a few stolen moments to relax and be extra nice to myself. Even if it doesn't work, I feel good about trying to lead a healthier life. That's got to count for something.

I often break the first rule of deep breathing which requires me to clear my mind of thoughts. I can do that for a few moments, but then a thought pops right in. Today was no exception. What if Janna and Jackie were right? What if I was being followed by Jeff's acquaintance? It just might be time to do some investigative sleuthing. I thought out my tactical plan and decided to get busy on it right away. So much for a healthy breathing exercise today! It lasted for about four breaths!

I began by recalling some of the details Jeff had told me and scribbled them down on my legal-size notepad. Her name was Shauna Green. She had worked at Trailhead Elementary School when they had gone on their one and only date. I already knew she had lived in the small town to the north of us. Even though Janna had said Shauna had gotten fired from the school, I decided to just call and inquire about her. As I was about to call, Officer Eric walked in the door. Eric was the younger policeman who had responded to my raccoon intruder. He had come to follow up on the break-in, and we had another good laugh talking about the "perp."

He asked if I had found anything else missing or damaged, and I told him about the car keys. Our lighthearted conversation changed a little for him at that moment. He told me that perhaps the raccoon had dragged them off but that I had done the right thing in changing the locks. Suddenly, I felt the urge to tell him about my car window. Now I could see a look of concern on his face. He said we should file a report. It could have been vandalism, and it would be good to have a record of it.

Okay, that seemed harmless enough, and I thought a good citizen should alert the police to any criminal behavior that might ever occur. He took out his notepad and wrote down a few details. Then he said the strangest thing. He wanted to know if anyone I knew might have any reason to vandalize my car.

"Of course not," I quickly replied, but then I thought of Shauna Green and mentioned her. His police training kicked right in, and I found myself asking him if he could check on one person for me. He readily agreed.

CHAPTER 7

The Arrival

Next on my wedding planning list of things to do was to settle on a venue. The problem was in our town, there were no venues. We didn't have a reception center or large hall or even an Elks Lodge. Jeff and I had talked this over a couple of times and still did not know exactly what we wanted to do. It was getting a little frustrating when one warm evening, we were sitting on Jeff's front porch, watching the kids play catch in the front yard. They both heard us talking.

"Why not have it right here?" Tiffany said.

We looked at each other, and suddenly the problem was solved. We would get married at the church and have a wonderful party right here on the farm. We could rent a big tent, some chairs and tables, maybe an archway or a dance floor and voila! Reception—done! I'd have to check with Anna and Tony to see if they would be willing to bring their generous gift of reception food out to the farm, but other than that, the rest seemed easy-peasy.

With the people, date, and place decided, our next task was invitations. It should be an easy thing to do. Print, address, and mail. Not much to that, but suddenly we realized that we knew just about everyone in town, and we had some extended family in other states. How many should we invite? Would people be offended if we kept it to a small circle of friends? How many refreshments would we need? It was getting rather complicated, and I thought I needed to do my breathing exercises. I could feel that tense, jittery feeling I loved to avoid at all costs. It made me feel a little depressed to think I was not enjoying the process as much as I was just ten minutes ago. It suddenly seemed like the perfect time to gather up the kids and head back to town. I felt like I really needed my eight to nine hours of restful sleep tonight.

Jeff seemed surprised that I so abruptly jumped up and said we had to go. I got annoyed. Geez, couldn't he see there were a million things to do and I was beginning to panic a little? How could he stay so calm? Maybe he stayed calm because he wasn't thinking of all the details and probably wouldn't be doing a whole big bunch of them and didn't have two kids to raise and a full-time job and so many decisions to make! The kids piled into the car, and they were chattering and laughing all the way back to our house. I was unusually silent, and that practically never happens.

After I got home, I got the kids off to bed, and then I soaked in a warm bath. I started to cry. Now this was weird to me. I mean, I loved Jeff, the kids loved Jeff, and he loved us. Logically, all was right with the world, but illogically, I was feeling like a tightly strung guitar string just about to pop! "Wipe those tears, little missy," I said to myself. "Tomorrow is another day."

Sometimes you just have to release those pent-up emotions, and then you begin to feel some relief. After crying in the bathtub and a good night's rest, I felt renewed. So off to work I went with a spring in my step. I actually noticed that I felt lighter today, not physically lighter, unfortunately, but emotionally lighter. I was determined to have a nice day. I had picked out a really cute outfit with dark denim jeans and a red and navy plaid blouse with tiny white daisy-shaped buttons down the front placard. My hair had been cooperative, and every girl knows that is a good omen for the rest of the day.

After a good meeting with the editorial staff and some good conversation with Janna and Rudy, I found myself happily writing baby announcements. It was definitely unusual to enjoy writing baby announcements. They were all so similar. I have found that a good mood can override many mundane chores, and today, it was baby announcements. Right about the time of this realization, our local florist shop van appeared with a pretty bouquet of *big* red roses. These roses were impressive with a deep red color and the look of velvet. I hoped they were for me, and in keeping with the happy events of this day, they were. They were not from Jeff, however.

Mr. Lawrence, the florist owner, brought them and asked if I would consider using his shop for my wedding flowers. He wanted to photograph the arrangements and use them in a new brochure and for future advertising. If I would use his shop, he said he would give me a big discount. Well, who could say no to that? I could check off another item on my wedding list. Flowers, done!

I was looking forward to my workday ending because Jeff and I were going to have dinner with Dr. Schott tonight, and I was anxious to hear of his progress in finding office staff and an expected arrival date. Dinnertime finally arrived, and just as Jeff and I sat down in Tony and Anna's café, we spotted Dr. Schott drive up. Jeff met him at the door, and they exchanged a hearty handshake and sat down at our table.

Anna was "on" us right away. She welcomed the doctor like he was a long-lost son returning from the war! Italians are like that. We can be pretty emotional about everything. It's part of our charm. We were not allowed to order anything. Tony and Anna wanted to bring us an Italian surprise, which literally means "tons of food!" We happily agreed.

Dr. Schott wanted us to call him Steve, and we started having an interesting conversation. He had pretty much wound up his business in the city. Most of his patients had been referred to other doctors that he felt would be right for them. He had packed up most of his belongings. He had also ordered the basic equipment that he would need to get rolling in his new office. It was all due to be delivered next week, and he would be here to set it all up. He said he had hired a receptionist but so far had not found a full-time back-office nurse. He had hired Denise Young as a part-time nurse, but she couldn't work full-time as she had two little children and also helped her husband with his construction business.

Oh, I was so tempted to say, "Hey, how about me?"

But I didn't need to as Jeff said, "You should hire her!" pointing to me.

Steve looked puzzled, and Jeff went on to say I had a nursing background and probably would jump at the chance. Before I knew what was happening, Steve was yelling, "Hired!" and we were all laughing. How could I do that? I already had a full-time job.

"How about evenings twice a week for a few hours?" Steve said. "And I'll try to find a third person to work the afternoons that Denise can't be there."

Suddenly I was a community news editor *and* a licensed practical nurse. I had no idea how this would work out, but I thought it would be fun to try.

The next morning, I sat down with my publisher and told him of my intentions to get another job two evenings a week. He had been so good to me upon my arrival in our town that I wanted him to know I was not quitting and would not short my efforts on behalf of the newspaper. He was completely supportive. What a good man he was! All his employees thought the world of him. Things were looking up in so many ways, and as usual, it's probably not good to get too comfortable with that idea because sooner or later, it's probably going to change. And boy! It certainly did.

CHAPTER 8

Dead Goats

It soon became obvious that a family meeting was needed to discuss our post-wedding place of residence. Attendance at family meetings is always mandatory, so we make sure we coordinate schedules carefully so everyone can attend and participate in the discussion. Plans and schedules were usual topics, but today we had an even more important thing to discuss. Where should we live after Jeff and I were married? We could all live in my current house in town. It was certainly big enough for the four of us and had the advantage of being close to the kids' school and school activities and everything busy teenagers needed. It was a mere five minutes from my office at the newspaper and my soon-to-be second job at Dr. Schott's office.

It didn't seem fair, though, to ask Jeff to give up living on the farm he had so painstakingly built over the years. His farmhouse had potential and was quite livable, even though I could think of lots of improvements we could make. It was peaceful and calm on the farm, and the animals always needed daily attention. What to do? This was the topic for tonight's meeting.

Tiffany was the first to offer her thoughts. She preferred to be in town during the school year at least, even though she loved the farm. Bryan thought living on the farm would certainly be a good reason he should get a truck to drive back and forth to school. I preferred living in town especially in the winter when snowy roads could be a problem. Jeff said either was fine with him, but he had the animals to consider. And then there was his job as a firefighter. It often took him out to a wildfire for days in a row. He had another rancher's son look after the animals during those days. He wondered if we would want to assume that responsibility when he had to be gone. There didn't seem to be any simple answer, and our first family meeting of the four of us left the problem with no resolution. We all needed to think about it.

Just as we were winding up, Jeff got a call. It seemed a rancher who lived further up the road from Jeff had just driven past Jeff's place, and he thought he saw two dead goats in Jeff's field. He had called Jeff right away. Jeff jumped up, and Bryan wanted to go with him, but I reminded him he had school tomorrow, so he reluctantly stayed home. "I'll call you," he said as he drove away.

Tiffany wondered how the two goats could have died. They always seemed so healthy and playful, jumping up on top of the wooden structure Jeff had built for them and flinging themselves off to the ground in great contortions. Goats, I thought, were kind of crazy animals.

It was a bit horrifying to find out later that night that the two goats were indeed dead, and there didn't seem to be any obvious cause of death. What in the world had happened to them? We just couldn't imagine. Jeff had called and said he would be taking them to the vet tomorrow to see if it could be determined as to the cause of their demise. For now, all we could do was try to get a good night's rest.

The following morning dawned clear and bright, and I sort of forgot about the dead goats. When I got to my office, I got busy proofreading several galleys of local news. Janna came in, and I told her about how we had tried to decide on the best place to live after the wedding and how our meeting had gotten cut short by news of the goats. Her eyes got wide, and I could see the wheels spinning in her head. What? What in the world could she possibly be thinking about our two dead goats? Just as I was about to ask her, Officer Eric came through the door.

He was certainly a pleasant person, and I admired his dedication to his town, family, and job. We were lucky to have him. He knew

Janna, and we all chatted for a few moments before he mentioned that "little matter" we had discussed. Of course, Janna's radar went off like a weather warning beacon. I almost saw the antennas come out of the back of her head! *She* should be an investigative reporter. Certainly, she had a nose for a good story.

I told Eric he could talk in front of Janna as she was my best friend and knew everything. Eric said he had done a little checking and found that Shauna Green had been dismissed from her teaching position as her behavior had become a little questionable and occasionally a little explosive. Some of the parents of her students had concerns. That did kind of fit the encounter I had with her in my office. Eric also said she seemed to be somewhat reclusive, and no one seemed to know her well. He had even talked to her cousin, the tractor salesman, and he said they didn't see much of each other. He could not, however, connect her to either of my incidents. There had been no neighbors or witnesses that saw anyone near my house.

Then Janna popped up and said, "And *now* we have two dead goats on Jeff's farm!"

Eric looked a little shocked at that remark, and I confirmed that two previously healthy goats had died at the farm just last night. So rather than closing up his notebook, Eric wrote down some information about the goats. He said he would check on that with Doc Joe. And with that, he was gone.

Janna turned to me. I knew what she was thinking. Could Shauna Green be responsible for the break-in, the shattered car glass, and the dead goats? Now that was a huge conspiracy theory based on practically nothing, but we both thought we should be careful around Shauna Green.

CHAPTER 9

The "Stalker" Revealed

Everybody in town wanted to help Dr. Schott get his office ready for patients. Jeff and I volunteered to help Steve set up his new equipment. They opened big cardboard boxes and were putting together chairs and tables of all kinds. Steve had decided on three exam rooms, two for adults and one for children. Jackie had signed on to do some children's wallpaper in the kids' room, and even with nothing else in there yet, it was so very cute. After the exam table with printed baby animal paper coverings, the little table and child-sized chairs, and two more chairs for parents, the room was nearly complete.

A small desk and a chair for Dr. Schott completed the look. It was so bright and cheery that just the atmosphere of this little room could make a sick kid feel better. The medical equipment company had delivered and installed the other exam tables, otoscopes, blood pressure monitors, and weight scales. Supplies filled the cabinets, and we installed a small refrigerator for medicines that required cooler temperatures. The children's room also had one small table with a scale to weigh the babies. Trish and her quilt shop buddies had made stacks of lightweight flannel covers to keep the baby's bare skin from the cold, steel bottom of the scale. It really couldn't get much better than that.

Each room was outfitted with the appropriate medical equipment, but in a way, that seemed like being in someone's home rather than a doctor's office. Janna had solicited some donations from our various merchants in town. The florist brought in several nice plants, and Mary Bundt's bakery contributed a prize jar filled with doctor-approved small toys and individually wrapped candies the receptionist could give out at the conclusion of a child's visit. Our hardware store had built a small bookcase and provided some children's books for the waiting room.

Mrs. Atwater and some of her friends donated handmade curtains for the front windows, and Danny's clock shop gave the office a nice big wall clock. These homey touches made everything look complete and welcoming. Dr. Schott, with his shirt sleeves rolled up and hands on his hips, beamed with pride.

Steve thought we ought to do a couple of days of training before the office opened for patients. So the following Tuesday evening found the doc and his employees converging at the office for filling out paperwork, discussing the record-keeping we would do, the billing system, and a tour of every nook and cranny of the office. Denise was the first to show up, and I came in a minute after her. I sat down to fill out my hiring information and didn't really look up until I heard the door open and the new receptionist's voice. It was none other than Shauna Green! Holy jumping lizards! I could not believe my eyes, actually, but here she was, all six feet and two inches of her. What had I gotten myself into now?

I looked up sweetly at her and said, "Oh, hello, Shauna. How are you this evening?"

She actually looked almost as shocked as I felt and replied, "Fine, just fine." Thank goodness Steve started talking right away. I was listening pretty closely, but honestly, I kept one eye on that Shauna person all evening long. Paperwork and training went on for a couple of hours, and then we all started for home. I was first out the door and first into my car and, without obviously speeding, got home as fast as I could.

Jeff was at the house with the kids, and they had just finished a big pizza. I was never so grateful for a big slice of cheesy pepperoni pizza as I was at that moment. Being there with the three of them made me feel safe and secure. Of course, they wanted to know how it all went, and I told them everything except the identity of the receptionist. I was saving that bombshell for Jeff.

After the kids went off to finish up their homework, I said, "Jeff! You are never going to guess who the receptionist is! It's Shauna Green!"

And do you know what he said? I mean, you just can't imagine what he said, can you? He replied, "Oh. She might be good at that."

What? After everything that had happened from our first encounter and Janna's theories, how could he so nonchalantly say that?

Well, I reminded him of every detail and said, "What am I going to do?"

He genuinely looked puzzled. "About what?" he asked.

I actually smacked myself in the forehead and leaned over right into his face and said, "What am I going to do about the maniac who may just be trying to kill me?" I know that was a little over the top; but what if, just maybe, it was her plan? Perhaps she had moved down the road from Jeff, broken into my house, taken my car keys, smashed my car window, killed two goats, and now was going to be working next to me in the nighttime, just waiting for an opportunity to make me disappear somehow so she could have a chance with grieving Jeff. Sounded plausible to me.

Jeff just laughed a little, and I pretty much determined I was marrying a guy who could not see the *big* picture at all! I could not wait to tell Janna in the morning.

It seemed that Janna had taken an extralong time to come into the office the next morning. She often would drop by a couple of our local stores before coming into our office to get their latest sale information or to talk about the following week's ad, but today, I wanted her to come right to work. She didn't.

Finally, she came through the front door. I jumped up and waved for her to come to my desk. "Good morning, sunshine!" she said, and then suddenly noticed I had a serious look on my face. I grabbed her arm and pulled her around the corner into the layout room which was now unoccupied.

"You will never guess who Dr. Schott's receptionist is going to be!" I almost breathlessly told her.

"Who?" she casually inquired.

"It's Shauna Green!" I squeaked.

I think Janna started to scream out something, and I put my hand over her mouth. "Shhh, don't let anybody hear this," I said.

Janna started to whisper something about this being a very bad thing and how all her worries were maybe right on the money.

Was Janna right? Did I have something to worry about? We talked a little more and then hugged and decided we should get back to work. But that little gnawing feeling of apprehension stayed with me into the evening that day.

CHAPTER 10

Medical Mystery

It wasn't long until Dr. Schott's office opened for patient appointments. We had put a well-thought-out notice into the paper which listed his office hours, his picture, and some of the kinds of exams he was offering. The very next morning, his appointment book began to fill up. My first evening at the clinic was only two days away, and I must admit I was a little nervous. It had been a while since I had worked as a nurse, but Dr. Schott was patient and thorough, and I felt comfortable working for him.

Jeff had taken on the task of staying with the kids on the two evenings I worked. They probably could have stayed by themselves, but I felt better knowing he was there and would keep Tiffany and Bryan company and help them if they needed it.

When my first night at the clinic came along, I felt ready. I bought a couple of sets of medical office uniforms. I didn't want to wear street clothes, of course, so some nice white uniform pants and a couple of tunic-type tops with big pockets made for a professional look. Those big pockets are essential to have as they can hold everything from extra pens to bandages and scissors. I put my stethoscope around my neck and my pen in my pocket, and I walked confidently into the clinic.

There she was, Shauna Green, sitting at her receptionist desk with the phone tucked under her chin as she wrote on the patient daily ledger. I smiled, gave a little wave, and walked down the hall to the part of the office that we had set aside for prepping lab work, storing supplies, writing notes, and discussing our next plan of action. We had a tall file cabinet and had designated the bottom drawer to hold our purses. I started to put mine into the drawer but then stopped. I decided to put it in the bottom drawer next to the sink. I don't know exactly why I did that. Perhaps I was just a tad overcautious that Shauna might do something to my purse or belongings. I got to work.

Steve came out of the exam room, and we had a quick discussion about who was in the room and why. And so it began. We saw about eight patients on our first night. It was mostly easy stuff like a stubborn head cold, an earache, a deeply embedded fence splinter, and a sore toe. I assisted Steve with whatever he needed to treat the patients. I must admit I sure enjoyed myself.

I walked out to the front office with the last patient of the night. After he had left, I turned to Shauna. "So how do you think it went today?" I asked.

We chitchatted a bit about that, and then Shauna said, "I'm so sorry I came into the newspaper office and yelled at you." She looked sincere.

I assured her I had forgotten all about it and that we should just move on. Even though that wasn't exactly true. I didn't want to let on that I was a little unnerved by her behavior and the weird things that had happened. She stared at me for a moment and then agreed.

*****

The next couple of weeks found Jeff and I finalizing our wedding plans. He was getting the hang of this party-planning stuff, and we were having quite a lot of fun. We set the time with the church and selected invitations and had them printed. We also arranged for a big tent, table, and chairs to be delivered to the farm, contracted a local DJ, discussed the flowers with Mr. Lawrence, and got the "thumbs up" from Tony and Anna to bring the food to the farm. Jeff had asked Bryan to be his best man, and Tiffany was my maid of honor. It was going to be a real family affair.

We also decided to live full-time in town at my house. It would work well for the kids, their activities, and my jobs. The farm was a mere ten miles away, and Jeff felt comfortable driving back and forth each day. He was training Bryan to take care of things if he had to be away, and as an "assistant farm manager," Jeff thought Bryan needed transportation. The day Jeff showed up with an older truck that was in good condition for Bryan, his wide grin and happy feet made us all smile.

It was the day after the truck excitement that some ominous news came our way. Doc Joe, our veterinarian, finally got the report back on our two dead goats. It turns out they had been poisoned! What? Poisoned? Really? Who would do such a thing? My goodness, we were living near goat murderers!

The toxicology stated propylene glycol. Jeff was shocked because he was sure there was none of that lying around the farm. Commonly known as antifreeze, he kept all that kind of stuff secured in a safe place in the garage. It was nowhere near the goats. It was certainly a mystery as to how the goats came in contact with that.

In spite of the felony goat murders, things were going along really well at the newspaper and at Dr. Schott's office, I thought. Wedding preparations were just about complete. We had decided to make our reception more like an open house where our friends could drop by and have a small bite to eat and celebrate a little with us. It was easy to pull together a guest list. I kept thinking maybe things were going along just a little too well.

One afternoon, Officer Eric came by the newspaper office. I was glad to see him because I had not had a moment to tell him what had killed our goats. Honestly, I had been so busy I kind of forgot about it. I could tell the information concerned him. He wrote everything down and said he was going out to the farm to look around. Right about then, his radio screeched, and he had an emergency call to get to. His investigation would probably have to wait for another day.

Only an hour or so later, I got a call from Steve. He asked if I could come in as early as possible tonight. It seemed Shauna had had some kind of wild temper explosion with a patient, and Steve had eventually sent her home. He was handling the office on his own for now but had a full slate of patients for later. I was able to get off a little early, raced home, changed clothes, and headed for the clinic. I called Tiffany to see if she could pull together the dinner I had planned, and she was happy to do it.

When I got to the office, luckily, there was only one patient waiting for the doctor. I checked him in, got my purse stowed, and checked our exam rooms to be sure they were all in order. Steve came out of exam room number one and was really glad to see me. He handed me the checkout sheet, and I saw that it was Mrs. Atwater who had had a dizzy spell today and was feeling a little "punk." That was a word my grandmother had always used. If you just weren't feeling your normal self, you were feeling "punk." I guess it was the word used in those days. Anyway, Mrs. Atwater was our punk patient today.

Eventually, we had a moment to discuss what had happened with Shauna today, and I could see Steve was very concerned about her. Apparently, she kinda snapped, yelled at someone, stumbled around her desk, and collapsed in a chair with a major headache. Steve had heard the ruckus, and he said she was definitely not herself. He checked her vital signs, did a neurological check, and all seemed normal. He had her lie down in one of the exam rooms. He wanted to run some tests, but she refused. She just needed to go home, she had said. Eventually, her symptoms subsided, and he reluctantly let her go. Steve said he was going to insist on running those tests tomorrow, and he planned to go by her place after seeing our last patient. I did tell him about her exploding at the newspaper, though, and he nodded and said, "Yes, tomorrow we need to do a complete exam."

CHAPTER 11

Coincidences?

The next morning at the newspaper office, things went along relatively well. Ads were approved for printing by their deadlines, and a variety of people had called to say they were bringing in announcements of all kinds in time to make our evening's edition. A strange thing did happen as we opened for the day, though. As people came in, most made some small talk at first, like how the wedding plans were coming along or commenting on how it was a nice day. Then they would lean over the counter and in a more quiet voice ask if I was still being stalked!

I would look at them with a shocked expression, and they would look around like we were sharing CIA intelligence or something. I would then quietly explain I didn't think I was actually being stalked but that a couple of coincidences had happened that just made it seem that way. I would assure them I wasn't concerned and they need not be either. They would nod slowly like we now shared a gigantic secret. "Be safe," one person whispered. Our rumor mill was obviously in excellent working order.

Now where would they get this information? It had to be Janna! I thought it was time for a soda break. I grabbed some change, got her favorite diet cola from the machine, and walked to her office. As I sat it down on her desk, she looked up with a startled expression. "What's wrong?" she asked with concern. I could see she really was into this conspiracy theory. "Look," I said, "several people have asked me about being stalked, and honestly, I am not worried about it. I don't think Shauna is doing any of that. I think it's all a coincidence."

Janna was nodding her head slowly back and forth. One of our advertisers had told Janna this morning when she stopped by that he was in the doctor's office yesterday, and the receptionist had blown up at him when he couldn't find his insurance card right away. That information convinced Janna that Shauna was just not behaving normally and certainly could be a stalker.

That information got me thinking. *Gee whiz...sometimes stuff just happens, and it seems like some sort of pattern. Those with wild imaginations will tie it all together in a neatly wrapped package and call it fact or truth.* The truth really is that it all just happened at inopportune times. That could be what had happened this time. But then again, what if the stalking theory was true? What if Shauna had a plan to do lots of little things that seemed odd, hoping I would obsess about them and it would someday make me go mad?

I tried to think about what I would be like if I became somehow unstable. I'd probably become undependable, irrational, mean-spirited, and goofy. I'd be late for work, forget to eat (well, that could be a bonus, actually), and would show up to the high school play that my kids were in, perhaps wearing my pajamas. I evaluated all that and determined I wasn't unhinged, at least not yet.

During my lunch break, I drove by the medical clinic. Denise was pulling double duty as receptionist and back-office nurse. Luckily, it wasn't very busy, and things seemed to be running smoothly. I walked to the back office and found Steve making notes on a patient's chart. After all the pleasantries, I asked about Shauna. Steve had stopped by her place last night, and although she seemed better, she still had a moderate headache. They had called her cousin, the tractor salesman, and he had come this morning to take her to the hospital for tests. Apparently, she did not want to go, but Steve insisted, and eventually, she relented. He had called the hospital with his test requests. It would take most of the day to get it all done.

Back at the newspaper office, another visitor stopped by. It was Mary Bundt. I was always so glad to see her. She was the perfect spokeswoman for any baking company. The love of baking was just "in" her. It was her gift, and everyone who could eat a little sugar was sure to never be disappointed. In her hand were some pictures of what she thought would be the ideal wedding cake for Jeff and me. And she was not wrong! I loved what she had picked out. Being the darling little sunshine baker that she is, when she asked me if she could make our cake as a wedding gift, I was overwhelmed with joy and love for this literally sweet woman. I mentioned that Anna was bringing some Italian cannoli, and Mary was so pleased with that. People could have cannoli or cake or both! Now that's a party!

As I was leaving the office for the evening, the sun was just beginning to set. Its last rays of this day made a beautiful show by bursting through a few puffy white clouds. I thought to myself how very blessed I felt to be who I am. I was the happiest with my job as a mother, and I had two regular jobs that were interesting and sometimes challenging and always necessary to our small town. And how wonderful it was to find a truly compatible companion in Jeff. He was a man who could take on a ready-made family as easily as one slips into a comfortable old robe. I also was lucky to live in a town with "my people."

What I mean by that is people who I loved and who loved me. They were people who helped each other and valued each other and lived in harmony most of the time. I liked the person I had become, the values I had selected, and the life I was leading. Yes, it was a perfect ending to a satisfying day. I didn't want my perfect day to end, but as it often does, things were about to change.

CHAPTER 12

Possible Explanation

On a very quiet evening, I sat at the kitchen table with my notebook spread before me. In it were all the critical details of the big wedding day, and I was carefully double-checking everything. I reminded myself I needed to drop off my deposit for our flowers to Mr. Lawrence. He was giving us a really good deal and was promising a profusion of flowing greenery with velvety, gigantic pink roses and waxy white stephanotis sprinkled throughout each arrangement. It was going to be beautiful.

Tiffany wandered into the kitchen and plopped down into the chair beside me. "Mom, I want to do a big project, and I need your permission and help." Thinking it would be something like the science fair or organizing the prom decorations, I readily agreed. "Sure, honey, what are you going to do?" I was unprepared for her answer.

"I want to redecorate the entire farmhouse! I already asked Jeff about it, and he said he thought the place could really use an update, and he is willing to help out."

I asked her what she meant by redecorating. I could see dollar signs piling up in front of my eyes. Tiffany told me it would be her big project for her home economics class at school. The teacher had asked each student to design a home; make a plan; pick out samples of all the materials needed for the project like carpet, tile, and paint; and make it into a presentation. That would be a fun project, but I suspected Tiff wanted to *really* do it! Leave it to my girl. She loved doing everything on a grand scale.

I needed clarification. "Do you mean you will make a plan, draw it out, and obtain the samples from various stores and shops?" I was afraid I already knew the answer.

"No, Mom! I'm gonna really do it, plan it, and then really *do* it to the farmhouse."

I was stammering and stuttering a little by then, and my response was a very weak "I need to talk to Jeff."

She seemed somewhat satisfied by that, at least temporarily. "Okay, but I have to tell my teacher about it by Friday."

I sat there, thinking just how much it would really cost to do a remodel or even just a redecoration of the house. With the wedding expenses and just day-to-day living, how could we possibly afford the project? It was probably twenty minutes later when I saw Jeff's truck pull into the driveway. I was starting to suspect he and Tiffany were ganging up on me with the plan to wear me down and get me to agree. It might be considered coercion in some circles, and I was getting ready to be the logical and financially savvy side of the discussion. I was *so* right!

Tiffany ran to the front door, calling out, "Jeff's here!" She seemed rather anxious to answer the door tonight. There were big hugs and little whispers between them as I walked into the room. They probably thought I wouldn't suspect their conspiracy to convince me, but my mother's radar was fully turned on and zeroed in on both of them. I did patiently listen to the fast-paced barrage of details from them both, and I could see they had already talked about this at some length.

I had to admit the idea held some interest from my point of view also. If we all were staying out at the farm occasionally on the weekends, it would be nice to make a few changes to the living situation. Single guys aren't the best decorators, usually, and while the house was comfortable and Jeff had done a pretty good job, there was room for improvement. But still, the money aspect was a worry to me.

It wasn't until Jeff told us that he had been saving for about a year or so for this very kind of thing. Knowing the house was getting older, he knew he would have to start replacing some stuff before too long, so he had started saving here and there in anticipation. How brilliant of him! I have to admit it sounded pretty reasonable and perhaps could actually be done, so I agreed to review Tiffany's plan with Jeff and see which parts we thought Tiffany could do. She was beyond-the-moon happy about it and scurried to her room to start the first drawings. As I stood there with my arms around Jeff's waist, I felt a little flood of happiness all around me. Life was going to be very good for us all, it seemed.

Later in the week, I went into the clinic to work my evening hours, and Denise was sitting at the receptionist's desk. "Where is Shauna?" I asked.

Denise, who was usually bubbly and smiley, looked rather somber. She asked me to come into the back office with her. Steve was standing there writing on a patient's chart, and he looked up, seeming rather concerned too.

"What's going on?" I asked.

Steve spoke first. It seemed the tests showed a small tumor in Shauna's brain. It was located in a delicate spot that was very near the portion of the brain that acts as an emotional control center. "They can't tell if it's cancerous or not without operating," Denise said, and she seemed near tears.

"Oh no!" I felt so badly for Shauna and a little ashamed of myself for thinking her behavior was just that of a slightly whack-a-doodle lonely lady. Maybe her behavior at school, in my office, and at the clinic was related to the tumor. Steve thought it certainly could be. Her surgery would be set as soon as the proper hospital team could be assembled.

The next day, I told Janna about poor Shauna's situation. While Janna was sympathetic towards her, it didn't keep her from still thinking about her theory that Shauna was obsessed with Jeff and a threat to me. I tried to convince her that it was silly to hold on to that. Shauna was in a terrible situation and could even die in surgery!

"Then where are your keys? And who broke your car window? And who killed the goats?" she demanded.

I had no answers.

CHAPTER 13

Not Buying It

Janna told our lunch group about Shauna's upcoming surgery, and everyone was rightfully concerned for her. She lived alone, eleven miles outside of town. We decided as a group to take on the job of caring for her as best we could following her hospital stay.

Jackie was the first to pull out her notebook and get a preliminary plan down on paper. She asked what could we do. Shelly mentioned that she had been out that way, driving her kids to a play-date, and noticed that Shauna's fence was falling down in a couple of places. She thought she could get her handy construction husband to fix that. In fact, Shelly wanted to give Shauna's place another look and see what else they might be able to do. She thought it would be a good family service project.

Since we were eating lunch at Tony and Anna's place, Anna was privy to our conversation. "Tony and I want to help too," she said.

I chuckled a little because Tony had no idea he had just volunteered for anything.

"We could make up single servings of our daily specials and freeze them for Shauna."

Hmmm, I thought. Getting a freezer full of yummy deliciousness from Anna was almost worth my getting brain surgery! What weird things I sometimes think about. Brain surgery was no laughing matter.

We all came up with a few ideas, and then our lunch break was up. Why does the workday go so slow, and the more fun part of a day sped by like a freight train? Anyway, back to the office I went. As I walked into my office area, I saw our publisher sitting on the corner of my desk, thumbing through a few typewritten pages. "Oh, there you are," he said. "I've got an article here about the Woman of the Year Award winner. Can you get it into tomorrow's paper?"

"Of course," I replied. "I'll take it right over to typesetting."

We chatted a bit about lunch, and I mentioned our plan to help Shauna after her operation. He thought that was a great idea. As he stroked his chin, he looked up toward the ceiling and then said, "How will Dr. Schott get along without a receptionist while she recovers?"

I had not thought about that. It could be a couple of months before she was well enough to work, and that's if everything went well during the surgery.

We both stood there, thinking about what that could mean for the whole town. There would be no one to consistently answer the phone, take messages, make appointments, file stuff, check people in, and deal with the most painful part of medicine these days, namely the insurance companies. "I know somebody who might fill in for her for a couple of months," he said. "I'll talk to Steve about it." And with that, he was out the door and walking up the street toward the clinic. Just one more reason I liked my little town. People knew they could help others, and they regularly did. I wondered, *What would it be like if the whole world was like that?*

Sometimes it seems like the day goes by so slowly, and it feels like forever before the time comes to clock out. Today was one of those days. Usually, my days seem to zip by with more to do than time to do it all. I felt my forehead. Perhaps I was getting sick. I didn't feel any obvious fever, but I found myself yawning, leaning back in my chair, and letting my arms hang down like a big silverback gorilla, whose hands were dragging on the ground. I came back to a previous idea that I definitely needed nine hours of sleep now instead of eight and had better seriously look into that new mattress.

So why is it that when a person has an "off" day, lots of abnormal things seem to happen? For example, I seldom spill anything on my desk, so of course, this day saw me spill twice! I generally pick up my feet quite well, thank you, but today, on this abnormal day, I caught my foot on the door threshold and actually took a tumble into the press room. This, of course, caused gasping and odd sounds to come out of a couple of my coworkers who helped me up. Luckily, I was not injured. And the icing on the cake this day found me answering the phone, spinning around in my chair to grab a pencil, and pulling the phone base off the desk and onto the floor where it cracked in three places! I was definitely having a rash of abnormalities happening to me.

When I got home, the craziness continued, but actually in a good way. Bryan and his friends were having a church activity night, and their plan was to play a kind of "run around in the woods" game followed by copious amounts of treats provided by somebody's mom. Since our house bordered the forest, it became a "home base" for the activity. That was just fine with me because I really liked all the boys and enjoyed seeing them have fun together.

About an hour or so into the festivities, Bryan and three of his buddies came crashing through the back door. "Hey, look, Mom! We found your car keys! Jax was running by those two trees that were knocked down in the big storm, and he just kind of kicked up the keys with a bunch of dirt and leaves. What are the chances of that?"

Sure enough, they were a little worse for wear, but there they were. So many things went through my mind, like I guess I didn't need to change my locks and waste that eighty bucks. And more importantly, Janna's theory of my stalker breaking in and stealing them could be put to rest. I was anxious to call her.

As I relayed the story to Janna, I noticed she was unusually quiet. I thought she would admit her idea of Shauna's obsession with Jeff and that I was maybe "misguided." She didn't. Instead she just said, "Well, what about the broken car window and the two dead goats?"

Oh, that girl! She was like a big old pit bull with a bone. No way was she giving it up. I washed the forest gunk off the keys and dropped them into the junk drawer. They weren't much use to me now, but I decided to keep them anyway.

CHAPTER 14

Take a Breath

The next couple of weeks were a whirlwind of activity. Tiffany started working on her renovation plan with Jeff at the farmhouse. They were busy every minute after school, in the evenings, and on the weekends. Jeff had only gotten called out one time for a small grass fire near the edge of town, so they had quite a bit of time to work on the house. They had decided I should stay away until it was complete, and it would be a big wedding surprise. I heard via the town grapevine that several others from the volunteer fire department were out there helping from time to time. Boy, was I curious, but I kept my promise of not going out there to observe the progress.

Also, Shauna had her surgery, and it had gone very well, and she was soon to be coming home to finish her recovery. Since her delicate operation had to be done in a very specialized hospital up north, no one except Dr. Schott had seen her. He reported she was making an amazing recovery. I was working as many hours at the clinic as I could to fill in the gaps in staffing coverage, but getting a temporary receptionist was certainly the biggest help. It turned out that Hank from the hardware store had a sister who lived most of the year with Hank and his wife. In her younger years, she had been an office manager for several businesses, and even though she was now retired, she committed to filling in for Shauna until she had finished her recovery. Her name was Lucy, and I really enjoyed getting to know her. She had that "can do" spirit about her, just like Hank, and the office ran pretty smoothly.

A couple of days before Shauna's release from the hospital, Steve asked me to meet him at Shauna's to check out the place, fill the freezer with Anna's frozen dinners, and assess if there were other things we could do to make Shauna comfortable. Luckily, Shauna had given him a key so he could keep an eye on things. I had embroidered two pretty pillowcases, and I bought two fluffy new pillows for her bed. I hoped she would find them comfortable and helpful upon her return home. It seemed lots of people wanted in on the plans to help out Shauna.

Mrs. Atwater, Trish, and the quilt group had made Shauna a beautiful lightweight summer quilt. Steve brought a walker from the office to help her feel steady on her feet. Mary Bundt had made a variety of cupcakes. Even Lucy, who had never met Shauna, had gotten a card for her and had patients who knew Shauna sign their best wishes for a speedy recovery. Dr. Schott was charged with delivering it all to Shauna's house.

Since Shauna's place was beyond Jeff's farm on the same road, I had to have Bryan drive me out there in his prized farm truck. He loved that truck and took really good care of it. I covered my eyes as we drove by the farm so as not to see any of the progress Jeff and Tiffany may have made. The small country lane could have used a fresh layer of pavement, but Bryan and I had fun bouncing along and singing at the top of our lungs.

I was unprepared for the sight of Shauna's place as we rounded the bend. The fence was standing up straight and had a fresh coat of white paint. Her front door was painted bright red, and it looked like the trim around the windows and doors had a coat of white paint too. There were pots of colorful petunias on the two front steps, and a welcome sign hung on the door. Bryan, Steve, and I hauled in our treasures. The house was really sweet on the inside, and with our additions, it was ready for Shauna's big homecoming.

In Steve's box, along with the food, were two movie DVDs from Jackie, and Shelly had her three girls make get-well cards. We set everything up, moved a couple of throw rugs that could be a tripping hazard, looked around, and pronounced it ready for the big day. I rode with Bryan back to our house with my eyes covered again as we drove by Jeff's farm. I *really* wanted to peek and almost did but resisted.

Shauna's return from the hospital went quite smoothly. Her cousin had picked her up and planned to stay with her for a couple of days to make sure she could handle being home and had what she needed. He told Steve she had been so surprised and pleased at the improvements and all the goodies that had awaited her. She also said she felt pretty good.

The day of our upcoming wedding seemed suddenly just around the corner. I checked my list of things to do and well, it looked like everything was done! It was only two weeks away. It was right about then that my nerves kicked in. As I looked in the mirror each morning, I would think, "Oh my! This woman is right on the edge. Look at her! Frantic, yes, that's the word. And is that a new wrinkle? What time is it? What shall I wear today? Clothes would be nice."

I was a bundle of crazy little snippets of anxiousness. *Breathe*, I would think, *but don't hyperventilate!* I never thought I would kind of lose a little self-control over my feelings, but I did. The good thing, though, was that I was as happy as I had ever been. And before I would leave the mirror, I'd say out loud, "Ain't life grand?" I had to admit, yes, it is.

CHAPTER 15

Secret Club Exposed

Having seen the pretty flowers on Shauna's front steps inspired me to add some of my own next to my walkway. As I turned over the flower bed dirt around a few of my larger bushes, I noticed a kid, maybe ten years old, standing on the sidewalk, watching me. I greeted him, and he seemed startled at first. I decided to investigate. I walked over to him. "So how are you today?"

Looking down, he stammered, "Oh, okay, I guess."

"Well, that's better than not being okay, isn't it?" I asked.

As I looked at his little face, I thought he looked like one of the Jackson boys. They were a nice family that lived a few streets over from us. "Are you Missy Jackson's son?" I asked.

"Yeah, I'm Billy."

"What!" I acted shocked. "That can't be! Billy was just a little kid about four months ago, and you are such a grown-up guy now. Are you sure you are Billy?" I said, winking at him.

He smiled just a little bit and then looked down, biting the corner of his lip. "I came to tell ya something."

Sensing this was difficult for him to do, I said, "Well, sure. Let's sit down and talk."

It was hard for Billy to get started, but eventually, he got rolling and had lots to say. "Well, my friends and I wanted to start a club. It was gonna be a club for just us five guys. A secret club. Hayden said he was the tallest and the meanest, so he was gonna be president. And

Hayden said we had to swear to never tell anybody our secret stuff, and we said, 'Okay, we swear.'"

I thought it didn't sound too bad so far, but then Billy continued, looking down, "Hayden said we all had to do something to show we were gonna be secret brothers." Billy paused for a minute and then looked up into my face, and he had big crocodile tears about to spill out.

"Why, Billy, you can tell me anything. I'll never tell a soul if you don't want me to."

Billy could hardly get the words out. "Hayden told us all the stuff we had to do. Andy had to take Mr. Henry's American flag from his porch and bring it to our secret hideout. Brad had to cut twelve of Mrs. Arnold's prize roses off her front bushes, and you know how that lady loves her flowers," Billy added. "And, and, and...*I had to break somebody's window to be in the club!* I didn't want to, honest, I didn't. But Hayden said I had to or I would be 'cast out' of the club." Billy went on, almost trembling now. "'Cast out' is just an awful thing, ya know. No one will ever talk to you again. That's what Hayden said."

"So it was you who broke my car window?" I asked softly.

As Billy burst into tears, I put my arm around him. "Do you want to know what I think?" I asked as I just continued without his answer. "I think Hayden is a terrible guy to try to make you boys do things you know are wrong. You and any other nice boys should form your own club and do nice things that make you feel good so you don't have to cry. You nice boys should get Mr. Henry a new flag and maybe take some cookies to Mrs. Arnold."

"But what can I do for *you*?" he asked as he dug deep into his pocket and pulled out some coins. "I just got my allowance, and you can have it all!"

"No," I said, "you keep that. I'd rather you wash all the windows on my car and make them all clean and shiny. How about that?"

Billy readily agreed, and I got a stool, the window cleaner, and some paper towels for him, and he got to work.

I kept digging in the dirt and watched as Billy carefully and completely wiped all the dirt and spots from my windows. "Can I do the inside too?" he asked.

"Sure, the car's unlocked," I called to him.

When he got finished, he came over to me. "I cleaned 'em all! They are pure sparkly now!"

"Doesn't it feel good to do the right thing?" I asked. "Remember, friends who want you to do wrong things really aren't your friends."

"*Boy*, that's the truth." He grinned as he gave me a big hug and ran off down the street.

With my flowers neatly planted and my car windows perfectly clean, I walked into the house to call Janna. I just had to tell her the broken window crime was solved. And in typical Janna fashion, she was so glad to hear that. "But what about the goats?"

She was certainly getting a lot of mileage out of this conspiracy, wasn't she? I told her that I was sure the reason for the goats' demise would surely reveal itself at some point. Actually, I was apparently almost psychic.

CHAPTER 16

Final Puzzle Piece Fits Perfectly

It was exactly one week before Jeff and I were to be married. As much as I was looking forward to that day, I almost wished it was all over and we were just an old married couple. Tiffany told me she and Jeff had finished her "remodel" of the farmhouse. She had already taken pictures and turned in her project to her teacher one day before the deadline and only one week before school let out for the summer. They had been cleaning up the outside a little this past week, anticipating our open house reception. All that was left was for Jeff to move that old tractor out of sight and put it behind the lean-to in the pasture.

Bryan was then going to mow the front property to the perfect height for our tent and guest tables and chairs. But tonight was going to be "super special," Tiffany said. They were going to do the big *reveal!* I was going to see the house for the first time since they had begun their work.

I have to admit I was excited to see it. I had imagined all kinds of things like Jeff would want dead animal heads all over the living room wall or giant antlers in the mud room to hang coats on or a cowhide in front of the fireplace. None of that would fly with Tiffany or me, thank goodness. But then Tiff might want a purple chair by the fireplace and a shiny ultramodern standing lamp next to it, and that would not fly with Jeff. This was going to be interesting.

Jeff was standing on the porch as we drove up, and I got that little flip-flop in my heart when he looked up and smiled toward our car. I found myself hoping I'd always get that feeling when we'd see each other, even one hundred years from now. Tiffany put on her tour guide hat and announced she would be doing the commentary. Well, okay then. This is exactly what she said. "First, please notice the fresh coat of creamy Highland White paint on the porch railings and window shutters. It complements perfectly the new striped cushions on the porch furniture. The poppy-red pillows add a splash of delightful color and coordinate with the red flower pots adorning the entrance. Please also note the welcoming red door and seasonal door mat. Won't you step inside?"

I am not kidding! My soon-to-be eighteen-year-old daughter had become a thirty-something interior designer and tour guide. As we stepped in, Bryan made sure I knew he had done the painting of the railing and shutters. Got it!

I gave a little gasp as I looked about the first floor of our sweet farmhouse. It was the perfect blend of everything I liked, everything I thought Jeff would like, and just perfect to accommodate all four of us. The old wooden floors had been sanded and finished so beautifully. A massive wooden mantel had been added to the tall stone fireplace. A heavy wooden side table sat between two matching overstuffed chairs across from a big leather sofa. Tiffany's signature accent throw pillows were strategically placed. New window blinds hung on every window.

While every room had a little something done to it, the kitchen was the true masterpiece of the project. This was the major improvement Jeff had been saving for even before I met him. This room was truly delightful with two new windows above the sink, new cabinetry and countertops, and most importantly, new appliances. Tiffany had done the tile backsplash, a skilled learned from Jackie while finishing the medical clinic before Dr. Schott's arrival. Bryan had sanded the kitchen table and chairs in his woodshop class, and his teacher helped him put a rich, dark finish on it. The new windows had gingham tie-back curtains. Only Tiffany knew that gingham was a favorite fabric pattern of mine. I had done her nursery in pink gingham all those years ago. I got little tears in my eyes when I saw them, and we hugged each other tightly.

We went from room to room, and Tiffany continued the tour, pointing out the little touches she had thought of. Truly, it was just delightful. Not one dead animal head in the place. I would be so happy to spend family time here with Jeff, the kids, and maybe, someday, the grandchildren. Really, can one person get any happier?

Finally, the tour ended, and we plopped down on the new porch furniture. I really could not compliment the three of them enough. They were all beaming. And then Jeff said, "Hey, Tiff, you know how you wanted me to move the tractor behind the lean-to in the pasture?"

"Sure," she replied.

"It was kind of an eyesore from that pretty kitchen window," Jeff continued. "I knew it had not run in a long time. In fact, it had sat there since I bought this place, about seven years ago. I thought I'd just have to drag it off with my good tractor."

I was kind of half listening because I was wondering why people just didn't get rid of old rusted-out farm equipment. A lot of them seemed to think these rust buckets were yard ornaments—the more, the merrier—but I thought they were scrap metal ready for the junkyard. Then I heard Tiffany and Bryan both yell, "Really?" all at once. *What, wait, what did I miss?*

Well, it seemed that when Jeff went to move the old thing, he saw something dripping from a rusted-out part. I thought, "Well, yeah…duh!"

He got under the tractor and found it was the old radiator that finally had cracked apart. And what was dripping out ever so slowly? Antifreeze!

"Did you ever have the goats back there in that part of the field?" I asked.

He said he had to think about it, but he remembered that he indeed had moved them to that area for a little bit to give the goats some new places to graze and let the grass grow more in their normal area. He had thought it was entertaining to see them standing on top of the old tractor and hurling themselves off in typical goat fashion.

At some point, though, they must have found the antifreeze drip and licked it up. Poor things.

And there it was. The final puzzle piece of our sleepy town's latest conspiracy had been revealed. The rumor of someone stalking me or someone's obsession with a former acquaintance could be put to bed. No one had been following me, stealing my keys, breaking my window, or killing our goats. It was all just a coincidence of events. I called Janna when I got home, and we had a good laugh. I'd have to call Officer Eric in the morning, but for tonight, I think I was going to sleep really well.

RUMOR 3

CHAPTER 1

Back to Normal

The wedding came off with barely a hiccup. I say "barely" because I have come to always expect one thing to go a little off the rails at every event. If it happens, well, I expected it, and it isn't as big a problem. If it doesn't happen, I count it as a happy freak of nature, not meant to be this time.

The day was a lovely one, not too hot and actually quite comfortable for the middle of summer. The tent we had rented provided perfect shade, and with its open sides, a slight breeze wafted through. The ceremony at the church was sweet and romantic with Mr. Lawrence's bountiful bouquets of pink roses surrounding our little family. Tiffany looked like an angel, and Bryan looked like a handsome prince, and I am not being biased because I am their mother. They really did look like that to me. Jeff was beaming and thoughtful and gentle and practically perfect in every way. And me? Well, my hair did exactly what I wanted it to, and that was just part of a super sweet day!

Actually, I was really pleased with how it all had come together, but mostly, I was pleased that our family was now complete. The kids now had a loving and full-time dad in their life. I had a real companion who treasured us the way we treasured him. And Jeff just slipped into both roles with ease. Anna and Tony's Italian food and Mary Bundt's wedding cake were mouthwatering and wonderful, and our friends and families got to witness the beginning of a new and happy life for us all. Probably my favorite moment was our first dance as husband and wife. An Italian cousin of Tony's, who also composes some beautiful music in her spare time, had written and recorded a love song just for us. It was titled "Sogno Calabrese," and I felt like I was in Italy surrounded by *amore* and there was only Jeff and me in the entire world. Neither of us could have imagined a better day.

Of course, fairly quickly, real life crept in on us all, and we had to start living everyday life. The kids were working this summer and trying to save money for the next phase of their lives. Tiffany had decided to take some classes at our community college and was toying with a few ideas regarding a possible career in interior design or business. Bryan was practicing for his last year of high school football and learning all about our farm, the crops, and the animals. I could see him going into the agriculture or ranching side of life.

Jeff had become the chief of our volunteer fire department and was promoting a plan to the mayor and City Council about making the fire department a full-time, city-sponsored entity. Our town was definitely growing, especially since it had been named the best little city in our state. We needed a real fire department with better and more modern equipment to serve and protect our residents. It looked like it just might happen if the budget could support it. I was back into editing the community news for the newspaper full-time and a little part-time nursing for Dr. Schott.

At the paper, we expanded our staff to include an assistant sports editor and a full-time photographer. Rudy was getting older and had probably attended a million sporting events over the years and could certainly use a helper. Dave turned out to be a recent college graduate with a love for sports, and he thought assistant sports editor was a dream job to begin his career. With the new baseball field hosting lots of high school and community tournaments, it seemed a game was always happening.

Dr. Schott had enthusiastically taken on the role of the high school team doctor, and he eventually decided the town needed to have a physical therapist. He began an internship at his office in conjunction with the college. It was amazing how busy the therapist actually was. It was often a pulled muscle, a sore arm, or a spasm in someone's back that kept him rubbing and stretching his patients and teaching the right exercises. One of the adult exam rooms became the therapy room. With football season about to begin, we were sure to get even more cases of sprains and injuries, and that didn't even count the inevitable farm accidents and mishaps that just always occur every year. There was seldom a spring or summer where someone didn't get kicked by a horse or cow, fall off a ladder, or slip and take a fall. It's just life on our planet.

I did notice one interesting little factoid this summer that had not occurred in previous years. We had quite a few out-of-town people coming into the newspaper office, asking for directions or information much more often. Most were guys who looked like businessmen, and I kept thinking they were sizing up our town for some kind of future plans. In my mind, that could be a good thing or a bad thing. Most folks loved our hometown just the way it was, but we could use a few more services, like the fire department or a small hospital. I just didn't want any expansion to ruin what we had going here, and from what I usually read or heard, expansion could be painful.

It was around the dinner table one night that my worries about expansion took on a new dimension. Jeff had casually mentioned that a sign had gone up on the north end of Main Street that advertised sixty acres of the Taylor's farm up for sale. I was so surprised! Margie and Ben Taylor and their family had run a big cattle business for several generations in that area. Their land ran from the edge of Main Street all the way up into the foothills, at least. Their bright white farmhouse sat at the base of the foothills, and with a big barn tucked into the expansive nearby pasture, why, it was just an idyllic setting. Who would sell off part of that? What was happening that would get them to sell? I should get Janna to nose around and see what she could discover.

CHAPTER 2

The "Smell" of Success

The following day started off pretty perfectly. I woke up to the smell of delicious bacon. Really, does anything smell as good as bacon in the morning? I know there are vegetarians out there who probably gag at the thought, but for a carnivore like me, bacon was the ultimate desired sensory overload. I like the thick sliced bacon with the peppered edges, sizzling and spattering in the big cast iron fry pan. A cardiologist might think I have a death wish, but alas, no. I just have a love affair with bacon. The only bad thing about bacon is the top of the stove when you are done cooking it. In my mind, the elbow grease to clean it up is well worth it.

Today was especially nice because Jeff was cooking the bacon. There he was, my tall, strong "I can do anything" kind of guy in his Wrangler Jeans and a denim work shirt and my ever-so-cute ruffled apron tied around him, cooking bacon. I never saw a more mouthwatering sight. I slipped up behind him and wrapped my arms around him and whispered the ever-romantic adage, "Mmm…bacon." It was the start of a great day.

At the newspaper office, I busied myself turning on lights and arranging the counter, which somehow seemed to find a way to get cluttered between the time we would close one day and open the next. Everyone passing through thought it the ideal spot to leave a box of office supplies, their coat, or a stack of junk mail that really just needed to be tossed into the garbage bin. Since I was usually not the first person to report for work each day, and some time had passed for the counter junk to start piling up, it often fell to me to straighten it out. I didn't mind, though, as my habit of being clean and organized, which was a curse and a blessing, kept the office generally welcoming.

Janna came in shortly after me, carrying some large proof pages for Labor Day sales that would soon find their way into our fall promotion section. She plopped them onto my clean and organized counter with her purse and sun hat and sat down in the chair across from my desk. "So what's up?" she asked.

Right away, I mentioned the land for sale at the edge of town and asked why she thought the Taylors would sell after all these years. Janna's eyes widened a bit, and she sat, contemplating for a moment.

Apparently, she had no idea and then said, "I don't know! But I'm going to find out!" And with that, she gathered her pages and purse and left her hat lying on the counter. I walked over, picked it up, and hung it on the coat tree in the corner. I guess I had two kids at home to pick up after and several more at my office.

Lucy was still our receptionist at the clinic and was doing a really nice job of filling in for Shauna. Shauna was recovering well from her surgery and gaining strength every day, but it would be maybe another month before she could return to her job. Today was one of my evening shifts, and as luck would have it, Ben Taylor was walking out with Dr. Schott as I was walking in. After some warm greetings, I casually mentioned that Jeff had seen a For Sale sign on part of their property. I hoped they weren't moving. Ben shot a sideways glance at Steve and said no, they weren't moving, but he didn't offer up any additional information. I thought that was a little odd, but we had two patients waiting, and I needed to get busy. Maybe Janna would have more luck.

As I was looking at our patient list for the day and evening, I noticed that Stevie had come in with his dad for an appointment. Oh gosh, I hoped he had not fallen off a ladder while cleaning someone's windows. He was such a nice young man. He was just a little quirky, and it was sometimes hard to get his attention and just as hard to keep his attention. He was a curious fellow, though, and often seemed a million miles away.

After greeting Dr. Schott, I asked about Stevie's visit. He told me Stevie had scraped his arm on an old nail on a window frame, and it bled pretty well for a bit. His dad had brought him in to see if stitches would be required, but just some butterfly bandages did the trick. He did need a tetanus shot, though, as it had been a good ten years since his last one.

I mentioned to Dr. Schott that Stevie was such a nice guy, just kind of all over the place and hard to talk to for more than two minutes. Dr. Schott said he had noticed the same things and wondered if perhaps Stevie had an attention deficit disorder. He went over to his big desk and called Stevie's dad.

His dad relayed how Stevie didn't do very well in school, even though he was quite bright. He just couldn't seem to concentrate. He got into a lot of trouble with his teachers, apparently, and except recently, when he was painting or cleaning a window, he seldom sat still until a job was finished. Dr. Schott suggested the idea of ADHD and wondered if Stevie could be tested. Stevie's dad asked if there was anything that could help him if he did have that condition, and Dr. Schott was quick to tell him yes. Great strides had been made in that area, and Dr. Schott thought they ought to check it out. Stevie's dad agreed.

As I stood there, watching this caring, thoughtful doctor, I felt so glad he had come to our town. What if there was something that could help Stevie have more focus and feel more peaceful inside? Wouldn't that be wonderful for Stevie? Dr. Schott was flipping through a phone book, obviously searching for something specific. "Aha! Here it is," he said. "I thought I remembered seeing an ad for a new clinic that does this kind of testing. And it's only about thirty minutes north of here." He wrote down the number and said he was going to call them in the morning.

We got back to business, and even though we only had a few patients scheduled this evening, three others came in, hoping to see the doctor. It all worked out, eventually, and we finished up only a little later than usual. As I drove home and turned the corner toward my house, I caught a glimpse of the house and how it looked at night from the outside. Some lights were on inside, which gave a golden glow to the windows. I sat in the driveway for a minute or so and thought, *This is what a happy home looks like.* Boy, was I glad I lived there.

I guess my headlights had turned on a sign inside the house that said "Mom's home. Attack!" I barely turned off the engine before the back door flew open, and Tiff was yelling something at me and waving a couple of papers. She wasn't crying, so maybe it was good news.

As I opened the car door, I heard squeals of delight, and she came running around the front of the car and plowed right into me. "What is going on, Tiffy?" I asked.

"I got in! I got in!" she replied.

"To what? What did you get in to?" I asked, and a scowl came over her face; like how could I *not* know?

"*Mooom!*" She could drag out my name really well. "I got into the design program at the college!" And she proceeded to tell me that they only take twenty students into the program each year and that the work she had done at our farmhouse was probably the thing that cinched her admission, and she was over the moon excited. She said I should look at these papers right away!

"Yes, yes, I will, honey. Let me put my purse down."

I barely caught a glimpse of Jeff standing in the kitchen, watching us with a giant grin on his face. She must have already attacked him with her news, and he was getting a chuckle out of seeing me be the focus now. Tiffany was jumping up and down and then bending over like she had cramps or something. "Calm down now, sweetheart. Let's take a look." And so the evening went on with Tiffany's continued squeals and very fast talking about what this could mean for her future and how she was meant to do this kind of work and how miracles still happen and one had happened to her because over 150 students had applied and she had gotten selected. And then, finally, about forty-five minutes later, she collapsed on the couch with the papers clutched to her chest.

Jeff and I looked at each other with little smiles and didn't move, not wanting to say anything that would spin her up again. We were going to give her a moment to bring her blood pressure back into the normal range and her pulse rate down below one hundred! It really was a miracle that her sweet, pretty head had not popped off.

After a few moments of calm had passed, Bryan strolled out to the living room. "Hi, Mom," he said so casually. "How was work?"

I marveled at him sometimes. Even with all the screeching and jumping and loud voices of delight in the house, he seemed completely unaffected. "Did you hear your sister's good news?" I asked.

"Oh yeah, sure. Great news. Can I have ice cream?"

I thought to myself, here are two kids brought up together by the same mom in the same house, and they are so different. That was actually one of the best things about having them both in my life. They each brought their own personalities to the table every day, and it made for lots of laughs and lots of hugs all around.

And how was Jeff doing with living smack-dab in the middle of our controlled chaos? Pretty well, actually. He seemed often amused, sometimes surprised, and occasionally stood there in amazement, waiting for me to explain the finer points of the current situation. He accepted it all and, in fact, seemed to revel in it. The rest of the evening wound down eventually, and sleep came easily to us all. Who knew what tomorrow could bring?

CHAPTER 3

The Plot Thickens

It was the fourth Wednesday of the month, so per our regular and never to be ignored schedule, my friends and I gathered for lunch at Tony and Anna's place. As usual, I was the last to arrive. It never seemed to fail that just as I was gathering my purse or sweater, the phone would ring on my desk or a customer would walk through the front door. Today it had been a phone call from the mayor's office to remind our publisher of his scheduled meeting with the mayor. I politely told the mayor's secretary I would be happy to remind my boss and asked her to confirm the time and place. I was intrigued as I learned they would be at the same place my friends and I would be at practically the same time! I wondered what they could be discussing as they seldom had lunch together.

All my gal pals were already seated and sipping on their sodas and munching on a few deep-fried mozzarella sticks. Anna knew what we liked, all right. Janna had ordered my soda, and it sat there in all its icy deliciousness, just waiting to quench summer thirst.

After hugs and hellos to everyone, we settled in to find out the latest from everyone. Trish was superanxious to share, and that was a pretty rare occurrence. So of course, we leaned in to pay attention. It seems she had gone on a "very nice date." She stated it quite matter-of-factly, and then she just looked around at our faces to gauge our reactions. Who, where, and when questions came from all of us.

Trish took great delight in our shocked looks. Well, it had been practically forever since lonely Trish had gone on a date.

I nearly fell off my chair when she said she had gone to a movie with Dr. Schott! What? He had not told me anything about that. I don't know why he would, really, but somehow I thought I should have known.

So the story went something like this. Trish and the quilt group ladies had made some chair cushions for the little benches in the children's area of the clinic's waiting room. Actually, I had noticed the little cushions, but I didn't know where they had come from and didn't think to ask anyone. Anyway, Trish decided to deliver them to the office, and she and Dr. Schott had gotten to talking a bit, and he asked her if she would like to join him for a movie on Friday night.

I thought back to the day I sort of accidentally started that first rumor in our town as an effort to give my single friend a little hope that someday some nice guy might come to town, and he would be "the one." Was it possible that might actually happen? I sat there, thinking I just might be the most psychic person in our state! Anyway, they had a nice time. The movie was good, and they both agreed to do that again sometime. Maybe a second date was a possibility, and that was a very good sign. Trish was just a bit aglow with this news, and we all were happy for her.

Jackie then piped up with her update. Her husband, Jack, had twisted his knee really badly and had been limping around for a week and complaining way more frequently than Jackie could stand. I suggested she bring him into the clinic tomorrow after he got off work when we had evening hours. She said he had been such a whiner she almost felt like making him walk there. In reality, she never would do that. Jackie was a real sweetheart, except perhaps if you happen to twist your knee.

Shelly was next to share. She said she was feeling a tiny bit blue because she and her husband had realized their three little girls were growing up so fast, and she wasn't enjoying the prospect of being an "empty nester." I mentioned how I hated that term, *empty nester.* It implies *everyone* has deserted their primary nest, and you are just left to wither away and die. So in an effort to make your last days tolerable, you just have to find some kind of activity or hobby or new circle of like-minded loners and try to squeeze a little more joy out of your life before you kick the bucket.

I think a new descriptive term for that would be so much nicer. Hmmm, maybe something like freedom lovers or if you were born in the baby boomers era, a name like boomers would be better. They both reflect a more optimistic outlook on one's golden years. I think everyone agreed.

Janna was next to catch us all up on her current projects. Right away, she said she had been busy investigating. As we all leaned forward, a hush came over our table. "Investigating what?" asked Trish in a whisper.

"Well, you've all probably seen the For Sale sign on part of the Taylor's property, right?" Janna asked.

We all nodded with eyes firmly affixed on Janna's face.

"Well, I can find no information so far as to why the Taylors would be selling any of their beautiful farm."

I mentioned I had seen Mr. Taylor, and he said they were not moving, and Janna stroked her chin a bit and got a more puzzled expression. "If a sold sign ever appears, I *will* find out who has put in an offer. I promise you that!"

Well, okay then. Let's move on.

I really didn't have a lot of news, except that Tiffany had been accepted into the design program at the college, and she was so happy. Everyone thought that was so terrific and wanted to wish her big congratulations. Everyone except Shelly. She had big tears well up in her eyes, and she quietly said, "They grow up so fast."

Janna slapped her on the back and told her to keep her chin up. By the time her girls went off to college, Shelly would probably be counting the days.

"Never!" she stated emphatically, but we all suspected it would probably be true.

About this time, my boss and the mayor walked in and sat down at a little table next to the window. The mayor was carrying some papers and a fairly large cardboard tube, the kind you roll up something to stick in there. Anyway, neither of them looked around, and Tony brought them a cup of coffee, and they began talking quietly between them. Oh boy! I wish I could be a fly on that window. I just had a feeling something big was going on. I could tell that Janna thought so too.

Our tummies were now really ready for the surprise Anna always made for us. Today was no exception, and she brought out plates of today's special. It was a creamy pasta alfredo with grilled chicken and a fresh bowl of salad for us to share. She set down a little bowl of freshly grated parmesan and looked quite satisfied that we all were just about drooling at the sight of it.

Tony's alfredo recipe had the secret ingredient of all good alfredo. His little sprinkle of nutmeg in the sauce made the dish perfect in my estimation.

Throughout lunch, I kept watching the mayor and my boss. Now they were unrolling the contents of the cardboard tube, and the mayor laid it out on the table. It sort of looked like blueprints, but it wasn't blue. I wondered, *Are blueprints always blue? Do they have to be blue?* Something to think about later, I decided. I just couldn't see what was on them.

I nodded at Janna, and she nodded back at me and started to get up. "I think I'll wash my hands real quick," she said. I knew she was going to pass the mayor's table on her way to get a peek. But right at that moment, the mayor rolled them back up and put them into the tube. Thwarted, Janna sat down. "Oh, I just remembered. I washed them right before I came." Nobody really thought much about it, but I knew what she had intended to do.

Lunch was delicious, and it was always fun to spend time with the girls, but we all went back to work or home with no more new exciting information than we had come with. Oh well. Maybe there just wasn't anything interesting in that tube anyway. It could maybe have been a drawing of new sewer lines or something. Eventually, we'd hear something if it was important.

That evening, around our dinner table, brought out some interesting conversations. Bryan was commenting on how dirty cows' behinds can be, and he asked, "Doesn't that bother the cows?"

Jeff started to snicker a little but then realized Bryan was asking a serious question. He then explained that cows were generally not aware of much, except eating and wandering the pasture. Bryan was sure that cows could not possibly ignore the smell, but Jeff assured him that they certainly could.

Bryan was rather perplexed at that answer. I sat there, somewhat amused because it seemed when we had boys around the table, most meals would have some mention of "belching, tooting, or pooping." Those, of course, were my sanitized words. Boys had at least ten other words to describe each part of these topics.

Tiffany first said, "Yuck!" and then immediately started to tell us about the first classes she had to take when college started in the fall. She wanted to know why she had to take English and Math and classes she had already taken in high school. That evolved into a discussion of "higher level" courses, being "well-rounded," and "transitioning into more adult interactions." She thought it was a big waste of her hard-earned money and that the college was ripping students off. Perhaps there was a little truth to that.

Jeff eventually mentioned that a Sold sign had gone up on the Taylor property yesterday. My head swiveled so fast it was nearly supersonic. Yesterday? Really? Yesterday? Why had he waited so long to tell me? He didn't know who bought it, so I would be telling Janna all about it tomorrow.

*****

It's actually kind of funny how many times I have rushed to work to put my head together with Janna and discuss the next big thing that was concerning us. We had a mental connection. I could almost always tell what she was thinking, and she usually could do the same to me. This day was no exception.

As Janna walked through the door, all I had to do was lift my head and look up at her, and she quickly dumped her purse on my desk and said, "What?"

All I had to say was, "It sold!"

And a gasp of air came from deep inside her. She pulled me around the corner of my office and into the hallway and began to tell me the results of this morning's investigation. Janna had been visiting some of our paper's regular advertisers as she often did before coming into our office. She leaned close toward me and told me *all* of them this morning had heard that a big discount store was going to be built there. The merchants were also very worried about how that news might affect them.

I agreed, knowing that often, these big chain stores came along and put the little guys right out of business. "What are we gonna do?" Janna whispered to me.

We just stared at each other, shrugged a little bit, and had to get busy with the day's work.

CHAPTER 4

Sugar, Anyone?

That night, as I lay in bed, unable to sleep, I began thinking about what truly would be in store for our town if a regional discount store was located here. The best case scenario was maybe a better selection of goods and maybe a lower price due to the bulk buying large chain stores use. Maybe some well-paying jobs for a team of people, including the older teens, might materialize. Those all sounded like positives, but then I started to think about the possible worst-case scenarios. What if the bookstore or the bike shop or even the quilt shop could no longer make a profit because people might settle for less quality products if they could get lower prices? What would our Main Street become if we lost even a third of our shops?

After all the work of our downtown revitalization project that had come about in hopes of attracting a doctor to settle in our town, what if that was all for naught as shops closed and empty storefronts lined the streets? The thought of that made me feel like I was experiencing morning sickness or food poisoning. I felt a few little tears on my cheeks. Oh goodness, that just can't happen in our corner of heaven on earth. I thought about Janna and the question we wrestled with in the newspaper hallway. What could we do? I really had no answer yet.

I must say I am not accustomed to having depressing thoughts that ruin my day, but the next morning, I just could not shake that ominous feeling of impending doom. I got all the way to my office before I could push the whole thing onto the back burner of my mind. But with Janna sitting in my chair, obviously waiting for me, I knew something was up. She jumped up as I came in the door and motioned me again into the hallway.

"Guess what?" she said, and without giving me a chance to give even a one-word reply, she went right on. "I ran into Harriet Gray at a church meeting last night. You know, she's the secretary at Jonathan Day's real estate office. I remembered that's who had put the For Sale sign up on the Taylor's property. I asked her who the buyer is, and she said she didn't really know. The buyer was listed with only the initials CDM Inc."

Janna stared at me, and my brain started spinning wildly. *CDM Inc.—what could that stand for?* It didn't seem to fit the big box stores I had thought of last night while lying awake. "Let's look it up!" I said and spun around to my desk and started to search on my computer.

And there it was! After bypassing the obvious well-known names, I saw one that could be it. Cutter's Discount Markets. It looked like a pretty big regional chain in our part of the country and seemed to have stores in most of the states around ours but only one store here which was in our state capital. I'd never been in one of their stores, but the name said it all. They would probably put more than a third of our shops out of business if they could sell all their wares at a discount. Oh gosh, why did they have to pick our town to expand in the state? That morning sickness feeling hit me again, and apparently, it hit Janna too. I think she gagged a bit. We both needed to quit thinking about it for now. It was already ruining our day.

I needed a distraction, so baby announcements and engagement photos and some local events got me onto other topics, thank goodness. When I looked up at the clock, finally, it was nearly lunchtime. I decided to take a walk up Main Street to Mary Bundt's bakery. Yep, sugar seemed the appropriate thing to eat on this day. I was going to have sugar for lunch.

As always, the shop smelled truly heavenly. I wondered, When people say something like that, do we really think heaven would smell like freshly baked bread, cakes, and cinnamon rolls? I didn't know for sure, but well, maybe. Jeff might think heaven would smell like steaks on the grill, and Anna would just have to smell garlic and sausages. Ha! I smiled to myself. Anyway, there was Mary, as cheerful as she ever was, loading up one of her turquoise boxes with a variety of cookies. She greeted me like the kind, dear person she always seemed to be and told me she was sending cookies over to the bank for their customer appreciation day. She looked at me and said, "Need some sugar, dear?" with a wink. She knew me well.

When people really *need* sugar, it's usually because some kind of stress has eaten up all the reserves of sugar in their blood, and their body needs a little jolt of sugar energy. The second possible reason is sugar is dang good sometimes. For me this day, it was both.

Mary picked up on my somewhat "off" mood and put a lightly floured hand on my shoulder. "What's bothering you, dear?" she asked. With very little prodding, I told her of my suspicions regarding the Taylors' land and expressed the worry I felt about our town, our way of life, and all the people who had made this place exactly the way we liked it. Mary's eyes opened wide, and I could see she was very interested in what I had to say.

Luckily, a homemade doughnut and a small glass of cold milk calmed my troubled heart, and I went back to work, feeling so much better. The rest of my day was fairly uneventful, and I actually left my office a bit early. I had planned a nice dinner for all of us for tonight and really felt like cooking today. That, too, is a funny thing to think about. I mean, why, on some days, is being in the kitchen like a jail sentence? On other days, it's the only place you want to be.

Luckily for Jeff, Tiffany, and Bryan today, I wanted to be there.

Bryan and Jeff came rolling in from the farm, and both needed a good scrubbing! I should never be surprised about that because any farm or ranch deals mostly with dirt, machinery, and in our case, chickens, goats, and stinky cows with dirty behinds. The corn was about four feet tall in the field, and the wheat was still light green, just beginning to turn golden. The hardest part of farming at this time of the year is making sure everything is irrigated properly and that weeds or pests have not adversely affected the plants. This year, we had four raised garden beds near the house full of healthy-looking vegetable plants.

Bryan brought home any veggies that were ripened enough. A couple of more weeks, and we'd have a bumper crop. He also would pick up the eggs that had been laid. He mentioned that there were "tons of cucumbers" on the vines. I hoped we could give most of them away. A few pickles and a few in a salad now and again was about all I could take of cucumbers.

I reflected on this happy scene of self-reliance and thought small-town, small-farm living was maybe the best way anyone could live. Tiffany came in about that time, and for the first time in her entire life, she asked what we were having for dinner because she was "starving." Truly, I had never heard her say that in her whole life! I could say that phrase about every three to four hours, but she said she seldom felt hungry and didn't even have a favorite food! How is that possible in a human? I had many favorite foods on any given day. I connected with seeds, plants, grocery stores, delicatessens, restaurants, bakeries, bake sales, cooking stores, pots and pans, grocery advertisements, snacks, and refrigerators. As Maria Von Trapp in *The Sound of Music* said, "These are a few of my favorite things!"

Dinner was a big success, and being together around our table and making plans for the next few days made me smile inside and out. Jeff was the "clean-up" crew every night with one or the other kids to dry his perfectly clean dishes. Oh, we had a dishwasher, but Jeff preferred to wash a lot of things by hand, and who was I to deny him this small pleasure? I curled up on the couch with this week's grocery ad and felt content indeed.

CHAPTER 5

Not in Our Town

The following day kept me pretty busy at the newspaper office. It was a really hot day outside, and I was appreciating the air-conditioning that was blowing a nice, cool breeze across my desk. Tonight was one of my shifts at Dr. Schott's office, and I was looking forward to the change of pace. When I arrived at the clinic, Stevie and his dad were just leaving. *What nice people they are*, I thought to myself.

Around the corner from the exam rooms, Dr. Schott was standing, holding up a large canvas, obviously admiring it.

"Whatcha got there?" I inquired as I stowed my purse.

Steve turned the canvas toward me, and there was a beautiful painting of our very own clinic. It featured our big tree, green grass, overflowing flowers surrounding the building, and even a little sign by the door that had Dr. Schott's name on it. The detail was amazing down to the little bird on a branch. The way the sunshine shone through the tree was truly picturesque. It was so professional and beautiful I bet people would love to buy it! It was really idyllic.

"Stevie did it for me," Doctor Schott said quietly and with a bit of emotion.

"Really? That is spectacular," I replied.

"It's a thank-you for helping him get his ADHD diagnosis and for how much better he feels on his medicine. He says he can concentrate and stay focused so much better. And his dad told me Stevie has been painting up a storm of beautiful artwork of many scenes around town."

"Fabulous!" I said, and then I had my first idea about the painting. "We've got to hang that right up in our front office," I said and started pulling open the drawers, looking for a hammer and a picture hanger. With no luck, I snapped my fingers and grabbed my phone. "I'll call Hank at the hardware store. He has a physical scheduled for tomorrow. I'll have him bring exactly the right thing."

Dr. Schott was used to my enthusiasm and so he just smiled and nodded his head in agreement.

Then I got my second idea, and it was a good one! Oh my goodness, when I get an idea, I just can't wait to make it happen. And this was no exception. What if I could find a venue to have an art show of Stevie's work? And what if I did a really nice article with photos for the paper? And what if some of the people at the capitol building got mailed that edition of the paper, featuring our local artist and his paintings? And what if the State commissioned him to paint other towns and businesses and landscapes and wonders of our State? And what if Stevie was able to support himself by doing something he loves? Oh wow! This, I determined, was going to be grand!

My evening shift sped by, and my thoughts kept returning to Stevie and his newfound abilities. Wasn't it truly wonderful that Dr. Schott had come to town and had been able to observe something in a patient that no one else had thought of and that he was able to truly help this patient in a very significant way? I also thought about how our doctor's arrival had affected so many of our residents.

Just in my circle alone, I saw Shelly get her kids treated easily for the myriad of sore throats and injuries they always seemed to have. I saw Jackie's husband get set up for some physical therapy for his knee, and Trish got to have a nice date. And I got to use my nursing license and do a part-time job I loved. Even though the idea of a doctor coming to town was just a rumor at first, somehow a whole lot of good things ended up happening. That's the way it goes sometimes.

I let my idea of an art exhibit percolate for a few days. One morning, I decided to get Janna on board. But before I could do it, Janna was anxious to tell me about a new rumor that was circulating as fast as an Indy 500 car on the track. It seems the town was going to have a big get-together at the park to see what could be done about stopping Cutter's Discount Market from coming to town. Janna said businesses up and down Main Street were really up in arms about it. Some were even mad at the Taylors for selling the property to CDM Inc. without any consideration of what it could do to other businesses.

"How did people even find out CDM was the buyer of the Taylors' property?" I asked her. She didn't know but said literally everybody knew about it. About then, our editor, Charlie, came by my desk and asked how we were doing, and Janna launched into the story of the community protest that was planned for Friday's noon-hour to stop the destruction of the best little city in the state! He was puzzled and shocked and wanted to know more. Janna was happy to tell him everything she knew. Charlie turned to me and said, "You and I better plan to be there to cover this story, and let's take our photographer too."

*****

When Friday rolled around, I was anxious to see what the protest would amount to, and I was surprised to see so many people there. They not only came to get information, but they came prepared, carrying homemade signs with slogans like "Not in Our Town" or "Don't Let Big Business Crush Us!" Some people carried colorful banners and flags. Hank, from the hardware store, was up on the gazebo platform and had a bullhorn. "Now, listen, folks. We will all lose our shirts if a big discount store moves in here. We need to let the mayor and the city council know that rezoning for such a store is not what the people want. And if they don't listen to us, we need to be prepared to vote them out come November!"

Everybody cheered and clapped and shouted out their approval. "We also need to tell the Cutter's Discount Market bigwigs to pick another city! We don't want 'em!"

More cheers and hoots followed that. "And that Sold sign just went up. We need to get the Taylors to reconsider who they are selling to. Are you with me?"

The crowd roared. We snapped pictures and scribbled notes for the article, which was sure to make the front page.

Right about then, from the back of the crowd, Ben Taylor himself called out to Hank. "Now wait a minute, Hank. You don't know what you're talking about here!" That comment was met with a lot of boos.

Ben was shouted down with comments like, "What are you doing to us, Ben?" and "This town has been good to you and your family. Just remember that!"

At that moment, Eric from the police department stepped up on the gazebo platform.

"Now, settle down, everybody! Just settle down!"

We were lucky to have mostly law-abiding citizens in our town that listened to Eric, but a few kept shouting, and Eric asked Hank if he could use his bullhorn. "Listen, everybody! You are starting to sound like an angry mob, and that's not who we are! Let's hear Ben out and see what the real story is." He handed the bullhorn to Ben who had made his way up to the front of the crowd.

"What my family is doing is going to be good for this town," he said.

More cries of disapproval filtered up, but Eric's stern looks quieted them a little. "I'd like to tell you more about the project but until everything is settled, I just can't. Can you just remember that I am your neighbor and your friend? Always was and always will be!"

I heard some grumbling like, "It sure doesn't look like it!"

Ben went on. "As soon as I can, as soon as the plans are finalized and the details are worked out, I promise I'll announce the whole project. Will you trust me?"

Well, that was hard for some people to do, but most remembered that Ben and Margie had been some of the first residents of this area, and they had supported every good thing the town had ever done. Most were willing to give him a little time. Ben assured the people that it wouldn't be long before everything could be revealed. He begged for patience.

Eric took over and calmly tried to disperse the crowd. People started wandering back to their stores or their cars, and a few stood around in small groups, continuing to wonder if they could really trust Ben. That was a tall order for some.

CHAPTER 6

Not Again

Since there really were no facts to print about the citizen's protest, Charlie decided to not run a story about it at all, at least not yet. No use stirring things up with just rumors. When there was something tangible to report, we would do a story at that time.

I thought maybe it was time to work on my idea for an art show of Stevie's paintings. And then I got the idea of why should we just limit it to Stevie? Maybe he would be our "featured" artist, but why could we not include the talents of others? Maybe more than just paintings. Maybe art in various forms from drawings to fabric art. Maybe a children's contest. What if we ran a coloring book kind of drawing in the newspaper, and kids had to cut it out, color it, give the character a name, and submit it to our office for a ribbon or prize? I really needed to talk to Janna, formulate a plan, run it by our publisher, and solidify the details. And I needed to talk with Stevie and his dad first of all. I made a few notes to myself and then got back to work.

Jeff and I and the kids were spending most Fridays and Saturdays on the farm, and it really became a most treasured break from our weekly routines. It was the weirdest thing, though, that I always felt like cooking a "comfort" meal when I was in my farmhouse kitchen. It might be meatloaf with mashed potatoes or my sausage and pasta casserole with a crispy green salad or maybe even Mexican noodles, which was a one-pan supper my grandmother had made for me many times as a kid. With my kitchen window looking out over the back pasture and a couple of cows wandering there, it seemed like meditation or tai chi could not have made me feel any more serene. And the cows were far enough out there that I could not see their dirty bottoms! My sweet Bryan had planted that visual in my head, and now it was certainly stuck there.

As we sat around the kitchen table for my "comfort" dinner, Jeff got a phone call. It was the mayor, and he left the table to talk with him. When Jeff returned, he was beaming. The fire department had been approved at tonight's city council meeting. It was going to happen! They had figured out a way to pay for a firehouse and four full-time firemen and would still train volunteers to assist. They were going to look into acquiring a bigger, better fire truck, perhaps secondhand from a larger city. It sounded like there was still a lot to figure out, but our town was going to have a real fire department. Jeff was practically giddy.

I decided to share the news about the big discount store possibly coming to the Taylors' property. At first, the kids and Jeff seemed excited until I mentioned how it could affect the economics of the Main Street shops and what could happen. Bryan got the most upset. "We don't need a store like that!" he said. "It will ruin everything."

Tiffany was less upset about that and wondered if the new store might have "cool" clothes or accessories. She was correct in knowing that our town was not a teenager's shopping paradise.

Jeff commented that Hank's hardware store would certainly lose some business, and he knew for a fact that some months were pretty tight for them already. Hank was always willing to help the farmers or local citizens and often let them pay on an installment plan for larger items. I was remembering how Hank and his employees had come through when we wanted to build the baseball field. What if that kind of community effort became a thing of the past? Suddenly, the table was quiet, except for the sound of forks on the dinnerware and an occasional heavy sigh from me.

And just like that, the rumor of CDM Inc. taking over the town started blowing up around us. Imagine my surprise when only three days later, an impromptu protest parade came walking down Main

Street, with banners and the high school band. Oddly, the protestors were mostly high school kids and their brothers and sisters. And leading the way was Bryan! A giant banner made out of butcher paper and held up by several of his friends read, "Save Our Town." The band was actually marching behind the banner playing "She's a Grand Old Flag" with the cheerleaders following and carrying American flags, waving them in the breeze.

I came out of my office and stood on the sidewalk as if the first astronaut on the moon had been passing by. Everyone was filing out of the businesses to watch. Many people cheered. Bryan saw me and gave me a big grin and a wave and flashed me the "We're Number One!" hand sign.

I thought, *Oh my goodness. He's got a "cause" to rally his troops around.* The battle had begun.

CHAPTER 7

Change Is a Good Thing, Right?

While CDM Inc. was the main topic on everyone's mind, I thought the art show might be a good, calming event the community could enjoy. I enlisted Janna's help, and we included Tiffany's assistance to make sure it was designed nicely and looked beautiful. Jackie came onboard to represent the mayor's office, and Shelly was to be in charge of the children's art display and project.

The first order of business was to contact Steve and Stevie. I went to visit them one afternoon. They both seemed very interested in the showing of Stevie's paintings. As Stevie showed me the depictions of the various parts of our town, I could see he really had an inborn talent. The canvases were alive with colorful streets, flowers, trees, buildings, and details I had never noticed. For example, instead of the straight-on view of City Hall, Stevie had painted the east side of the building where a small garden was located with a statue and plaque honoring the first settlers of our area. I'm embarrassed to admit I didn't even know it was there.

With one project still on his easel, he had about thirty-five completed paintings which took up most of the family's garage. Steve said he and Hank and employees of the hardware store helped to convert the garage into Stevie's studio. The family car and the window-cleaning truck were now relegated to the driveway.

With Steve's permission and Stevie's enthusiasm fresh in my mind, I went back to my office to put my head together with Janna and plan the promotion. We drew up our basic outline of where, when, and how and went into our publisher's office to get permission to sponsor another event. When he saw us enter, he leaned back in his chair and said with a smile, "Uh-oh! I see troubling coming!"

We all laughed. We decided to make the show a part of our Labor Day celebration weekend. That meant we had to get busy. Dave, in advertising, said he would make up a big display ad for our next issue. With a call to Jackie, plans to inform the mayor and city council were set in motion. Jackie also volunteered to contact our Parks and Rec office and reserve the downtown park and gazebo.

I gave Dave a list of the kinds of art we were looking for, and it was actually amazing how quickly it all was coming together. For a little while, we all kind of forgot about CDM Inc. and what that might mean for our town. That was true until the very next day when enormous earth movers showed up at the property where the discount store was rumored to be built.

For a few days, the giant equipment just sat near the road alongside the property, but before long, they began moving. As they started up, they belched big plumes of nasty black smoke as they slowly rumbled back and forth on the land, grading off the green pasture grass, and turning it into plain old dirt. It made me kind of sick to see it. Apparently, it made a lot of people sick, and most mornings, there were new placards jammed into the ground, protesting the building of Cutter's Discount Market. The pictures and letters to the editor were nearly a daily feature in the newspaper. So far, it was a "peaceful" protest, but one night, peace slipped away from our hamlet. Someone had spray-painted a few not-so-nice words on the equipment in giant orange letters. Officer Eric was now investigating a crime of vandalism. This store was causing problems before it was even built.

With fall coming shortly, I noticed a few leaves here and there in the trees turning bright yellow. Before long, our streets would be a profusion of reds, oranges, and yellows. The only bad thing about fall was that those beautiful colors didn't last near long enough in my mind. Why would God go to all the trouble of making those trees change to colors that could take a person's breath away and then have them fall off just a short time later? I wished these gorgeous leaves could stay on the trees for at least twice as long. And we wouldn't have to rake them up so soon either!

Dave's publicity for the "Art in the Park" event was as striking as our fall colors, and everyone was talking about it. People had to sign up with me at the newspaper office, and I would then plot a space for them based on the articles they wanted to show. Stevie, as our featured artist, was to have the entire gazebo and area surrounding the gazebo for his paintings. Our print shop was making a few posters to put up in shop windows, and Janna was giving them out. It would begin on the Saturday of the Labor Day weekend. Every artist was to set up their table or display by 9:30 a.m. Each of them was responsible for their own tables or easels or whatever they needed to showcase their contributions. They could sell their art if they wanted or just display it. I never knew we had so many talented people in our town as my list grew day by day.

It seemed everyone had something to offer. Mary Bundt was showcasing big, maple leaf-shaped sugar cookies in autumn tins. The quilt shop girls were to display their favorite quilts and had Christmas flannel pillowcases for sale. Mr. Lawrence of the flower shop was teaming up with the bicycle shop to offer a line of bicycle baskets decked out with showy autumn mums. The bookshop would decorate a small table in fall colors and show some winter reading selections with homemade fabric book covers and page markers. Some of the employees of the hardware store were going to show the metal yard art they had made. Trish signed up to show her watercolor paintings, and that surprised me because she had never mentioned painting as an interest of hers. See, you just never really know everything there is to know about a person, even if you've known them for a long time.

There were people who had knitted sweaters and hats, a man who made western riding saddles, and someone who embroidered holiday dish towels. Anna and Tony were displaying Italian holiday desserts and giving out little samples. We also had several people whose talent revolved around pottery and ceramics. With Stevie's art at the center of it all, it was sure to be a great show.

With such a fun event to focus on, the conversation about CDM Inc. died down for a while. But when some surveying markers with orange plastic ribbons began appearing in the freshly graded dirt, there was no denying a building was coming soon. There was really nothing that could be done about it. CDM Inc. had applied for a zoning change from agricultural to commercial, and the county had granted it even with a coordinated barrage of protest letters from town residents. I just couldn't drive by there without thinking it all was partly my fault. If I had not accidentally started that first rumor, no doctor would have come to our renovated town, and we would have never garnered enough attention to become the best little city in our state. And no big discount store would have ever even heard of us. Yes, I think I could take a lot of the blame for all of this.

Guilt is a weird thing, isn't it? No one is inflicting pain upon you, but it can really hurt. I was no exception, even with my generally positive outlook. It was harder to deep-down smile. My new hairstyle and cute outfits didn't help much. In fact, sometimes I thought I was a big old phony, like I had a mask on, and nobody could even see the real me anymore. I was indeed causing myself a boatload of unhappy feelings.

When a line of cement trucks started pouring the outlines of a foundation at the site, I literally cried. It was truly happening now, and I hardly dared to picture the future. I tried to push from my mind the picture of store after store on Main Street with big signs like "Sale! Everything Must Go!" and in small print below, "Especially that girl from the newspaper who ruined our town."

CHAPTER 8

Wild Guesses

The one bright spot on the horizon was the "Art in the Park" gathering. Practically every inch of our rather small city park on Main Street was filled with tables and easels and displays. I had to obtain some sidewalk space adjacent to the park to hold all our participants.

The day of the show turned out to be a rather glorious day, warm and sunny. Promptly, at 9:30 a.m., cars and trucks began to pull up to the park and unload their treasures. Within thirty to forty-five minutes, the park was transformed, and the crowd was beginning to grow. Atop the gazebo, Stevie and his family had all of his art beautifully displayed. There were already some sold signs on some of Stevie's paintings.

I was glad our newspaper's photographer had gotten there earlier and was capturing this special morning. It was another example of the joys of a small town with people greeting each other, exclaiming their delight at the various booths, and sharing a happy moment. And it was a very hot market, too, for all the goods displayed. Some vendors were even taking orders for items to be made later.

Shelly had done a wonderful job with the children's corner. She had picked the cutest picture of a Christmas angel for the children to color. It had run in the paper for several issues, and dozens of children colored in the picture and named the angel. All entries were received in my office. Shelly and I poured through them and found one particularly endearing. Little Nancy had done a great job at coloring and named her angel Kirsten. It was a clear winner. Nancy won a pair of feather angel wings and $5. She was thrilled.

All in all, the art show was a community success, and a front page layout the following week documented it all. School was about to start up for another year, and back-to-school ads dominated our newspaper. We pretty much knew where to get the needed supplies, but we always looked at the ads and made mental notes of who had the best ideas for this fall. The bookstore always had the best selection of book covers, and of course, some of the reading materials the schools required. The bike shop ran specials on bike racks and locks. But it was the hardware store that always made me laugh. Every year, their back-to-school sale was for ammunition. I'm not kidding! You see, back-to-school coincided with the opening of hunting season.

At first glance, you might think they were encouraging students to bring a gun to school or something. That's what I thought the first time I read that ad. In reality, they were promoting the opening of deer season. The longer I lived here, the more I came to realize that many, many families depended on that meat, and it was a serious business.

One particularly beautiful day, I decided to take a short drive out to the CDM Inc. building site and see what progress had been made. Even though I didn't really want to look, I sort of had to! Maybe work had stopped and the ground was already starting to grow back some pasture grass. Now that would be worth seeing. I pulled to the side of the road and sadly saw work was progressing. But I was puzzled too. The footprint of the building and the few walls going up didn't seem big enough to be a large discount store. They were paving a pretty good-sized parking lot, though, and I thought maybe it was like a first phase or something. It was curious. At the end of the parking lot, there were the beginnings of a couple of smaller buildings, and I thought maybe this was the home of the gas pumps that were sure to come. No signs were up announcing the opening dates or anything. Humph, I was stumped. *I'll ask Janna.*

I drove back to my office and cornered Janna. She had been by the site also and was convinced it was their small-town version of their big-city store. That would make sense, I guess. And maybe a smaller store would not hurt our businesses as much. Maybe. At least I could hope.

That night, as I walked into the clinic for my evening shift, I saw that Shauna was back! I was genuinely so glad. She had been through a lot and pretty much had to go through it alone most of the time. I hugged her and welcomed her back with sincerely good feelings. She looked healthy and said it had been a long road but that the brain tumor was gone and she was healed and feeling pretty good. "Still a little tired sometimes," she said, "but stronger all the time." We got right to work.

Just as I was about to head to the back office, Dr. Schott and two men came from his office out to the front. They were obviously friends, not patients, and they were laughing and making plans to see each other soon. Dr. Schott introduced me, and I found out they had all graduated from med school together and had remained good friends. From there, it was a busy evening with some interesting cases and time flew by.

I was tired when I got home. I wondered how long I could work two jobs. Maybe I was stretching myself a little thin. Oh if only "stretching" could make a person thin! That would be a weight-loss revolution! I could be a millionaire.

CHAPTER 9

Horses Can Solve All Problems

I decided to ask Jeff about the CDM Inc. construction. He had seen it and also thought it looked a bit small for the superstore we were anticipating. Just what were they planning? Were they going to "creep" into town and get on everyone's good side and then expand like a hot air balloon? Were they just building their garden center first to appeal to the agriculture-minded people of our area and then blast us with a giant expansion? I could almost see their underhanded, sneaky business plan in my head, and I was none too happy about it. Whenever the construction was mentioned, scowls came over the faces of almost everybody like a monster thunderstorm about to unleash golf ball-size hail. They were just going to ruin everything, and I couldn't get the thought of it out of my head.

So began the autumn this year. Everyone was having some kind of challenge, it seemed. At lunch one day, I learned that Shelly's girls were determined to not like their new teachers. Trish and Mrs. Atwater had butted heads over the order of new Christmas fabric. Was it to be traditional reds and greens or some new Christmas combination? Janna was having a problem with a sore foot from accidentally stepping on a good-sized stone right in the center of the arch on her right foot. It made walking all over town with ad copy pretty uncomfortable for her.

With Tiffany attending college and Bryan busy with his senior year, Jeff harvesting the wheat and selling off some cattle, and me working my two jobs, time just flew by. And so did the construction of CDM Inc. The building was nearly complete, and it didn't look like anyone expected.

How can I describe it? It was very farmhouse/barn-looking with two main entrances. That was clever on their part, I thought, to try to "fit in" to our rural atmosphere so customers would patronize them. Still, it wasn't very big, maybe only the size of a home furnishing shop or large gift shop. The two buildings at the end of the parking lot didn't look anything like a gas station either. Where were the pumps? I had not seen them bury any tanks. I was perplexed. After all, I worked at the newspaper for goodness sake! I'm supposed to be in the know! Everyone always expected me to know everything! Even my own family expected me to know everything.

What time was the game? Where would the nails be at Hank's hardware store? When were the Scotts coming back from their vacation? Stuff like that! Why did they think I should know all that? But certainly not knowing about CDM Inc. bugged me through and through.

I had to actually try really hard not to let this conundrum ruin my bluebird-of-happiness attitude that I normally have. Logically, it seemed silly to let this bother me, but emotionally it was another story. I decided I needed a break from thinking about CDM Inc. and wondering about it and maybe feeling a little guilty about it. I know! Let's go buy a horse! Everybody knows that having a big beautiful horse erases every bad feeling.

I could not believe how easily I solved my somewhat depressed mood. All it took was thinking about getting a horse! *Now that could be a new therapy*, I thought. *Anybody down in the dumps? Just think about getting a horse!* Any girl like me would be on top of the world in no time. I could not wait to talk to Jeff about it.

I got home from the newspaper just a few minutes before five and started prepping a big green salad. Bryan had picked *a lot* of lettuce and spinach from our garden, and the frugal gal in me wanted to not let any go to waste. There were a couple of cucumbers, three picture-perfect tomatoes, some green onions, and two yellow peppers. I always add a small can of medium-sized black olives and a handful of toasted croutons. Then I sprinkled some freshly ground parmesan cheese on top. A little olive oil and rice vinegar dressing, and voila! A delicious salad sitting in the fridge was now ready for munching. The rest of the meal would take a little more thought.

Bryan came bouncing into the driveway in his farm truck, and Jeff was right behind him in his own truck. They both jumped out and headed toward the house with Jeff playfully slapping Bryan on his shoulder and the two of them laughing out loud. Bryan had formed a solid relationship with Jeff, and the farm was the perfect place for them to build a real father-son relationship. Tiffany would not be home for dinner tonight as she had some big paper due in one of her classes. We'd definitely save her a nice piece of steak, although I suspect she would only want the salad.

Eventually, we sat down to eat that farm fresh salad and the steaks that Jeff had barbequed. It was right about then that I said, "I want to get myself a horse." As I looked at Bryan and Jeff, they both had stopped mid-chew and were looking wide-eyed at me.

"What?" Jeff asked.

"I want to buy a horse," I replied. I sensed I had their attention, and so I began my story. I had a horse when I was thirteen and was living at home with my mom and dad. She was a speedy little quarter horse, sorrel-colored, about four years old. She was only green-broke, which means you could probably count on her to not want you to ride her most days and that it took quite a bit of strength to control her and stay seated on her back. She didn't even like the gentler snaffle bit, her saddle, or even a halter. She did like to be brushed and talked to and told several times a day that she was the best horse in all the world. Her name was Lady Bug (due to her reddish color), and once I got her saddled up and ready, we often rode fearlessly up the mountain behind her pasture for hours.

I shudder to think of that today. Here I was, just thirteen, riding alone in the mountains on tens of thousands of acres of National Forest land with a rather wild horse, no cell phones, and no way for anyone to ever find me if sweet Lady Bug threw me off onto a tree and cracked my head wide open. It was a different time in those days. My parents didn't seem to worry at all, even when I told them some of the wild things that happened on those rides. Like the time Lady Bug and I came to a little ravine near the pasture border, and lying on the bottom was a scraggly-looking older man. I wondered if he was dead. He was lying very still.

I called to him, and he stirred a little. He kind of tried to get up and fell down again and slurred a couple of bad words, and I took that as an invitation to get out of there right quick. I rode back to the corral and told my mom, who I think told my dad, and maybe they called the police. I don't really know. I just turned Lady Bug in the other direction and headed up the mountain.

Anyway, riding along those forest service roads up to the giant water tank above town was an experience I wished everyone could have. It was quiet, just the *clop*, *clop*, *clop* of Lady Bug's hooves on the hard dirt trail. There would be an occasional hawk floating on a thermal updraft, just floating along without even having to flap his wings. One day, we came around a familiar bend on the trail, and Lady Bug stopped short and would not move. Her ears were perked straight up, and she was looking off the trail to the left. I asked her what she saw. I only saw remnants of a very large tree lying on the forest floor, pine trees all around, and a manzanita bush tucked in here and there. I tried to urge her forward, but she would not move.

And then I saw it too. Sitting on top of that tree on the forest floor was the biggest owl I had ever seen! He had to be twenty-six inches tall at least! He blended in beautifully with the surroundings. His camouflage was perfect. Hey, don't owls sleep all day and come out in the evening to hunt prey? I never expected to see this guy at ten in the morning! Anyway, I suddenly got concerned because if this big guy took off, Lady Bug was sure to bolt, and I could be sent flying. I shortened up my reins, squeezed tight with my thighs, and uttered a few comforting sounds. I nudged her with my boots, and she took a few tentative steps. We walked on up the trail, and the owl watched us the whole way.

During the telling of my horse stories, Jeff had gotten a chance to digest what I was saying. Being the supportive new husband that he always is, he calmly said, "Okay. That would be a nice addition to the farm, and there is certainly plenty of room to ride unhindered out there. Let me figure out the barn situation, and I'll need to build you a corral. It's probably best to put that on the east side of the barn where we have a water source already in place. And I'll ask around to see who might have horses for sale. What kind of horse are ya thinking of?"

And thus began a marathon conversation about what kind, when, how, possible price, etc. Bryan got tired of it all and went to our living room to watch a little TV just about the time Tiffany got home. She just ate the salad.

CHAPTER 10

Good Diversions

With my horse memories flooding my mind and the process of finding the perfect new horse to buy, I kind of forgot, for a moment at least, about CDM Inc. The building on the property was really taking shape, and during lunch with my friends, we all agreed that it was going to be a small version of the discount store we expected. Janna told us that many of our shop owners expected the new store to be ready around the beginning of the holiday season so they were planning their offensive moves right now.

For example, starting the first of October, the shop owners decided to stay open later on Friday and Saturday nights. Anna and Tony were going to offer antipasto plates and a glass of wine to hopefully entice a few more shoppers to the downtown area. The bookstore was reconfiguring a corner of the shop to be a "Meet and Read" section with several comfy chairs and footstools and hot coffee or cocoa. They would give a deep discount on books to curl up with on a cold winter's night.

Mary Bundt was going to offer a free holiday baking class in her bakery. I was going to sign up for that right away! Just like our downtown renewal project, most stores were participating in sales or specials each Friday and Saturday evening to try to boost their bottom line and to compete with CDM Inc. At the newspaper, we decided to run "Stop and Shop" ads that would remind people of the extended hours. We also were giving away free classified ads for the first ten people who placed a fifteen-word or less ad during the extended evening hours. This, of course, meant at least one employee had to work a couple of extra hours on Friday and Saturday nights, but we all decided to take a turn and figured we'd only have to do that maybe one time each during the holiday season.

One of the best additions to the downtown plan was actually put out there by the mayor himself. He found a little money in the park's budget to build a small ice rink in our little park, near the gazebo. It wasn't much, really, just a wooden border in an oval shape with a heavy-duty liner of some kind of plastic material. After filling it up with a few inches of water, Mother Nature cooperated by providing the freezing temperatures. Hank brought in a little firepit and a few logs for our opening night on the first Saturday in October.

The first Friday had been a fabulous, exciting night as Bryan's football team had played a hard-hitting game against their biggest rival and had won in the final few minutes of the game. They were now in the playoffs toward a championship. In a small town, almost everybody goes to the games. It's a good, family thing to do, and we were no exception. Bundled up in our warmest gear, you could see every breath we took. We put down a blanket on the metal bleachers and zipped ourselves into our sleeping bags. They became the best way to contain our heat. We huddled as close as we could, which was a real pleasure for me to be next to Jeff. After the game, with excitement still in the air, people mingled downtown for a while, visiting the shops or just standing around, talking. It seemed like everyone was anticipating the opening of the ice rink the following evening.

Saturday found our family catching up on necessary chores. It seems like Saturdays ought to always be a "play" day, a rest from regular work, and a day to do something else—something fun. It seldom seemed to work out that way, though. It became more of a catch-up day. It just doesn't seem fair, does it? Anyway, eventually, the winter delivery of firewood got stacked, and we counted that as our Saturday exercise program. Extra groceries were bought, too, considering the kids wanted to meet friends at the ice rink and make smores over Hank's firepit.

By the time the sun set, and the lights of our downtown came on, we were all kind of tired, but we pulled it together and headed for the park. Truly, it was a smashing success. A few kids were already on the ice, and some people were strolling around, looking in store windows and taking advantage of the "Stop and Shop" specials. I closed my eyes to listen to the evening. If you have never done that, I highly recommend it. In the middle of an event, just close your eyes and listen. It's kind of an amazing thing. You can hear a child's precious giggle, the little rocks crunching under the tire of a car, and the faraway swooshing of a breeze in the treetops. It's like a whole other world, really, one that gets a bit blotted out by wide-open eyes.

I thought I'd check in at the newspaper and see if anyone had taken out a classified ad. Diana had volunteered to work a little later and was at the counter. "Any takers?" I asked.

"Yes, and I'm really surprised," she answered. Six people had come in to place their free ad, and the night had hardly begun.

I walked out of the office and headed back toward the park. I sure had mixed feelings inside. The downtown was bustling, well, as much as any small town's downtown could bustle. And people looked content and happy, except for that kid that just took an amazing spill on the ice. He definitely wasn't happy. But overall, the promotion seemed to be accomplishing exactly what we'd hoped it would to support the small businesses and have some fun doing it. But then I remembered the main reason we came up with the idea in the first place. It was really to remind everyone not to forget our little town and not to "sell out" to the big business that would soon move in and maybe change everything. Even twinkling white lights on the gazebo at the park couldn't chase away a sense of dread of what might lie ahead.

CHAPTER 11

New Addition

Jeff, the angel that he is, had finished the preparation at the farm for the arrival of our newest family member. She was a really pretty palomino mare, about four years old, who needed a new home and a girl like me to hug her and tell her how wonderful she was. Jeff's firefighting friend had a friend who had a sister who needed to find a good home for a horse that was a bit too spirited for her. I had been anticipating her arrival for two weeks and spent the time getting all the necessary equipment I might need to help her live a happy life at our farm. I had also been reading up on training a horse and hoping some new techniques might make it easier. And I wanted to come up with the perfect name for her. I read somewhere that animals respond best to two-syllable names. My friends and family were *no* help at all on this score.

Jeff thought Goldie was a good name. That was too common for a golden-colored horse. Tiffany thought Sunshine fit, and it wasn't a bad choice but didn't feel quite right. Bryan offered up Thunder because of the sound her hooves would make on the ground when she was in full gallop mode. That seemed like a boy's name to me. Janna thought of Buttercup, but that was three syllables. Trish thought of Dolly which seemed too young for my mare, and Shelly was sure this horse should be Spirit because she was, well, spirited. Jackie said she had no opinion and didn't want to make that kind of decision, and I thought she had been working in a politician's office too long!

In the end, it was up to me, and I chose Blondie. With her golden body and blonde mane and tail flowing in the wind, Blondie seemed just about right. Blondie's former owner delivered her to the farm while I was still at work. Jeff called to say she had arrived safely and was exploring her new surroundings. I could hardly wait for the end of the work day so I could drive out to the farm and see my big girl and begin a little training.

As I neared our farm, I noticed my heart was beating a little faster than normal. Yep, I was excited! And then, just over the rise, was our sweet little farmhouse. I pulled up to the front steps and rushed from the car into the house. Jeff didn't answer me when I called his name, so I hurried to the kitchen to look out the window toward the barn. That's when I saw her. Really, she was breathtaking. She was standing in the little corral Jeff had built next to the barn with him calmly brushing her shiny coat.

Jeff saw me coming, and a giant smile broke out on his face. Blondie saw me, too, and her ears perked up, and she looked intently at the approach of another person. "Oh my goodness," was all I could say. Now I'm not one that gets really emotional about stuff. Oh, I feel things deeply sometimes, but it doesn't really show up like glistening eyes or quiet sobs. That was *not* the case today. I truly was overcome, and as I climbed over the corral fence and moved cautiously toward her, she gave a soft little exhale of horsey breath. Yes, I was now officially in love—with Jeff, of course, but also with Blondie.

I reached out to her, and she eyed me shyly at first. I took the brush from Jeff and ran it down her long, golden neck. Jeff gave me a little kiss on the cheek and started back to the house. I stood out there for quite a while, just brushing and talking to her and telling her she was about to have the best life any horse could ever hope for. As the sun was now definitely giving its last little bit of light, I opened the gate and let her into the pasture. She tentatively took a few steps toward the gate, and with a little encouragement, she stepped into her new world. Tomorrow I would ride her, and I knew we could become partners in our adventures. What a contented feeling I had.

CHAPTER 12

Weird Coincidences

Really, if you have never had a cherished pet, you just can't understand how an animal can become such an important part of your life, and absolutely *no one* at work could understand my excitement at getting a horse. What was wrong with everybody? I had looked at their pictures of children, nieces, nephews, new furniture, new cars, and food recently eaten at some fancy restaurant on their last trip. Was it too much to ask them to "ooh" and "aah" a little bit over my horse? I mean, after all, this was a living, breathing new addition to my family. Besides that, she was so beautiful. It was much more interesting than that giant hamburger Dave got at the advertising luncheon. Oh well, they couldn't see it, and it bugged me a little at first, but in the end, I just figured they didn't know what they were missing.

Even though it was often getting chilly by the time I got off work, I found myself more than occasionally driving out to visit Blondie and maybe take a short ride in the moonlight. She was learning how to anticipate my commands and really was a quick study. She had her own mind, though, which I actually love in an animal. It's so great to see animals think and have ideas of what they want at some particular moment. Blondie often wanted a full-blown gallop up our dirt road that runs past the house, and I was happy to oblige. That little bit of carefree wild abandon made any less-than-happy moments fade from memory. Yep, getting a horse had been a truly brilliant idea.

Back in town, I sometimes had to face a little reality head-on, and some days, it was actually pretty hard. Being the community news editor meant I always wrote the obituaries, and this week, Arnie died. It's kind of a shock when someone you hear from regularly or see often around town is just not there anymore. Finding out Arnie had died made me think of the times he called to complain about the bowling scores not being in the paper that week. Since he and Mrs. Atwater had become friends, he called my office a lot less. I thought how she would miss his voice which was never gruff with her.

I have to admit I cried a bit while writing his obituary. The funeral home had gathered the information from some family members, and I put together a really nice life story for him. We had a picture of him at the new baseball field on opening day with a grin as wide as can be. I decided to appreciate each day with Jeff just a little bit more.

It's odd that bad news often comes in threes. Number two was that Tony had a stroke! Anna told Jackie, and Jackie told Janna, and of course, Janna told me, and I was heartsick. How often Tony had made something special for our lunches at the restaurant, and Anna delivered it to our table, beaming with pride over her husband's fine Italian cooking. Janna said it was a mild stroke and he would be okay, but Tony was going to be in the hospital for a couple of days. Anna was with him, at his side as usual. We arranged to send him some flowers. Janna was going to check on what we maybe could do to help with anything at the restaurant, like meet a delivery truck or something.

Bad news number three was a big banner at the discount market construction site that merely said, "CDM Coming Soon! Don't Miss Our Grand Opening." That sign was a stab in the heart. Arnie was dead, Tony was in the hospital, and now the monster store, CDM, was going to ruin our whole town! I really needed a few hours with Blondie to make sense of any of this. I left work a little early, put on my warmest coat and boots, saddled Blondie, and headed up the dirt road. Today she just walked along, not even a trot, not even a head toss. I think she sensed my mood and was just there to be my steady friend. Tears streaked my cheeks for most of the ride, and Blondie seemed to listen to my sad story all the way.

CHAPTER 13

The Big Reveal

Winter was steadily pushing in on us. The last of the fall leaves had been raked up, except at the Jenkins' house. I really couldn't believe it, but it was another year of them *not* raking a single leaf! Soon enough, I guess, the strong winter winds would pile them up against their garage or send them down the street to some field. The teens saw more evenings cold enough to skate at the rink as it was frozen pretty solid after the sun went down. Tiffany was enjoying her college experience so much and loved feeling her creative senses awaken in her classes. Bryan attended the Winter Formal which was his first big dance where he asked a girl. Not one for a lot of dating, he mostly "hung out." From what I could tell, "hanging out" was a bunch of boys and girls who were just friends, who went to games or movies or parties together. Being serious with anyone didn't really fit into the "hanging out" part, and I was glad about that. My sweet little kids were already growing up way too fast to satisfy me. If I could have kept them younger, I think I really would have.

Jeff was so, so busy these days with the construction of the new firehouse and the calls the fire station would get from time to time. Usually, the calls were not major fires, but what an excellent service they provided when someone had some trouble. There were sometimes minor traffic accidents, an occasional out-of-control barbeque fire, or a farmer who was burning a pile of weeds that got going a little more than it should. Luckily for our town, we had no major events for the department, and Jeff hoped we wouldn't, at least until the new equipment the city had ordered could arrive.

Jeff kept busy with training and staying at the ready. His "free" time often revolved around the farm. It seemed that all of us kept a pretty busy schedule.

Things at the newspaper and Dr. Schott's office were always interesting and varied from day to day. I was really enjoying my jobs and my life until one day, Janna burst through the front office door, dumped her pile of stuff on the counter, and called out in a loud voice, "Well, it's finally happening! CDM is opening next week!"

"Oh no," was all I could squeak out. I had been by the building site several times with hopes of seeing into the building and gleaning more information on exactly what kind of store they were planning. The windows had been completely covered with brown paper on the inside and, well, it all seemed rather mysterious. I never caught a big semitruck delivering stuff either. They had to be sneaking it in at night, I thought. There was a fairly big stone structure out by the road that was to hold the store's new sign, but no sign had yet appeared.

At Dr. Schott's office, his two med school buddies were huddled up together in the back apartment where Steve had been living since the office opened. When I poked my head inside, all three jumped a little. I asked them what was going on, and they fell all over themselves, saying, "Oh nothing, really. Just visiting" as they scooped up the papers they had been pouring over. It all seemed a bit suspicious to me, but we had patients waiting, and Steve's two friends filed out rather quickly. What was going on? Something was up, I was sure. We had an interesting night of patients, and by quitting time, I had mostly forgotten about the meeting in the back room.

The next day at the newspaper, the mayor strode in with a big grin on his face. He wanted to see our publisher and editor. That was another odd thing, I thought. When they went into our editor's office and closed the door, I was a little miffed. *How am I supposed to hear anything if they close the door, for Pete's sake?*

After about fifteen minutes, they all came out, laughing and smacking each other on the back like they had just won a gold medal at the Olympics. Okay, now, things are just getting a little too weird. I asked Charlie what they had been talking about and if he knew what was said.

"Wouldn't *you* like to know!"

"Well, *yeah!* That's why I was asking!"

He wouldn't say a peep. That called for two diet sodas and a trip to Janna's office to relate how I was being kept out of the loop about something.

The next weird thing was Dave and Charlie had their heads together, creating a rather large ad for tomorrow's paper. When I saw it myself, I got that sinking feeling again. It was an ad inviting the community to the ribbon cutting that would celebrate the opening of CDM this Friday at 3:00 p.m. No other news than that!

I was determined to be in the front of the crowd and see just how bad the damage was going to be. I didn't sleep well that night or any night, and when Friday rolled around, I was dead tired from my self-imposed sleep deprivation. But there was no way I was going to miss the big event.

Jeff came over from working on the firehouse to pick me up for the ribbon cutting. I was somewhere between being really mad about the whole thing and really sad about the whole thing too! People had already begun to congregate in the parking lot in front of the store, and there was a big gold ribbon strung out from two of the front pillars. I saw the mayor drive up and noticed the big sign by the road had been installed and was covered with a sheet and tied up with the same gold ribbon. The brown paper had been removed from the windows, but the glass was tinted dark enough that I couldn't see in.

Officer Eric and his partner were there, keeping people in the parking lot a little ways back from the building. It seemed like most of the town was filling the area now, as curious as Jeff and I were. We heard some grumbling residents who had already decided not to ever patronize this CDM store, not ever. Some were very skeptical, and the atmosphere was tense.

Precisely at three, the mayor stepped to the podium. After two squeaks of the microphone and a couple of taps, he began to speak. "Ladies and Gentlemen," he began rather dramatically. "Thank you for coming. Today is a momentous day for our fair town. We are no longer the little hamlet that we once were."

I heard a couple of people mumbling pretty loud about that and saw Eric shoot them a slightly stern look.

"That's a good thing," the mayor continued. "Growth has made it necessary to expand services within our borders. For example, you have probably all seen the progress we have made on our new fire station. Let's give a round of applause to Captain Jeff and his team for their tireless service." The crowd quickly agreed. "And now we have another expansion that will help all of us. I'd like to introduce the three men who have made this possible!"

The entrance doors of the building slid open, and to everyone's surprise, Dr. Schott and his two medical school colleagues I'd seen at the medical office several times came through the door. They were dressed in sharp, white lab coats and were waving to the crowd. The crowd was stunned but began some tentative applause. "Steve," the mayor said, "will you give us some details about this project?"

Steve stepped up to the microphone. He began, "First, I'd like to introduce my friends, Dr. Johnathan Hadley and Dr. Daniel Kent, who have been committed to this project for some time now. And I'd also like to thank the mayor and the publisher of our local paper for all the time, effort, and help they have given us. And mostly, I'd like to thank Ben and Margie Taylor. Without their generosity, we could have never been successful."

Everyone was thoroughly confused by now. Could all of these people have conspired to ruin all of our businesses and our family-friendly town? That seemed impossible. Steve continued, "I know there has been a lot of talk about CDM Inc. around town."

A few boos rang out from the crowd.

"But I'm here to tell you CDM is here to stay!" You could have heard a pin drop. "CDM stands for Caring Doctors of Medicine. My colleagues and I have been planning and working tirelessly to bring a fully staffed twenty-four-hour medical clinic to our neighborhood, and here it is! We will have an urgent care facility with laboratory and X-ray capabilities. No more driving fifty miles north for these services. We will also have a clinic office for Dr. Hadley, who specializes in internal medicine, Dr. Kent, whose specialty is emergency medicine and trauma, and of course my own family practice office."

Everyone was gasping now and looking at each other with the shock and awe usually meant for the largest of happenings. I caught Janna's eyes, and they were almost popping out! Trish was there in the front row with a happy grin. Jackie stood by the mayor, and both were surveying the crowd with satisfaction. Even Shelly and her three girls were there, and Shelly was clutching her chest as if she knew she was going to be using *all* of these services just to get her girls to adulthood.

Steve went on, "You are probably wondering, why all the secrecy? Well, I have to tell you, there were many times when we thought we could not pull this off. We truly didn't want to get people's hopes up and then disappoint our neighbors. This facility was a huge undertaking for three guys without much business background. I mentioned before the generosity of the Taylors. Well, if they had not donated the land, we could not have obtained the financing to build this place." Spontaneous applause burst forth, and I saw a couple of men slap Ben on the back like they had known this the whole time.

"What you see in front of you is actually only the first phase. To the east of the parking lot will be a large pavilion, which will be used for a permanent Farmer's Market which will showcase and sell all the terrific things that our farmers and gardeners grow. We, as doctors, want to encourage the eating of healthy, farm fresh products. It could also be used for larger community gatherings as we are close to outgrowing our little park downtown. There will be a small obstacle course, playground area, and walking trail in the front part of that pasture behind the pavilion."

"What about those two little buildings to the north?" someone yelled out.

"Glad you asked," Steve replied. "The Taylors are turning that area into a farming education section. They plan to offer tours of their working farm and activities that might help our children appreciate and continue our farming and ranching traditions. Ben and Margie's kids and some of their grandkids will be running a farm and ranch animal petting zoo with educational instructions on caring for the animals and their surroundings. They may eventually be offering the opportunity for kids' field trips from their schools. This would be open for more than just our kids. We hope to get schools from towns around ours to consider visiting."

Everyone was grinning now, it seemed.

Steve continued, "You know, folks, when I first came to our town, I didn't really know what to expect. You have all been so welcoming, so kind, and so helpful to me and your neighbors. Your families are strong, and that's what we doctors like to see *and* to have ourselves. Dr. Hadley and Dr. Kent are moving their families here shortly. Our own special people are here today. Let's welcome them!"

The audience burst into applause as Dr. Hadley's and Dr. Kent's wives and children came forward and waved to the crowd. Steve held out his hand and gave a little wave to Trish, and she stepped forward too. He took her hand, and she gave him a quick kiss on the cheek. Jeff and I looked at each other, and he gently closed my mouth that was hanging open about a foot!

Well, that evening, I was still reeling from all that had happened. I thought back to that moment when I accidentally started that very first rumor about a professional coming to town and everything that had happened since. As the sun was setting, it found Jeff and me sitting on our front porch, looking out over our little farm. Having our home in town and coming out to the farm regularly had surely changed our lives and the kids' lives too. I could truly say I felt blessed our family got to be part of the best little city in the State. I can't imagine being anywhere else.

ABOUT THE AUTHOR

Family life touches so many emotions from humor and excitement, joy and wonder, to shock and awe! Author Nancy Oleksy likes to focus on the positive side of life and the relationships that make her life rich with excitement and adventure. From this perspective, *Rumor 1, 2, 3* was born. Based loosely on the real-life experiences of the author as a community news editor in a small town, she weaves a tale of "Any Town, USA" and the personalities of residents who choose to live there.

Nancy grew up in Lake Tahoe, California, became a nurse, and married her forever partner, Bob. Together they have loved and laughed around the world while Bob served in the United States Air Force and worked for Boeing Aerospace. They have two wonderful grown children and six grandchildren they adore. Currently retired, they live in Eagle, Idaho.

"I hope I have never actually started a rumor," Nancy says. "But if I did, I would hope it would work out just like it has in *Rumor 1, 2, 3*."